nh

Fyodor Dostoevsky (1821–1881) was born in Moscow, the son of a physician, and educated at the Military Engineering College in St Petersburg. His first novel, *Poor Folk* (1846), was well received. In 1849 he was arrested and sentenced to death for his involvement with a group of Utopian Socialists, the Petrashevsky Circle, only to be reprieved at the last moment. His experience of four years of hard labour and imprisonment in Siberia led to a profound change in his ideology. This is reflected in all his subsequent fictional masterpieces, from *Notes from the House of the Dead* (1862), to *Crime and Punishment* (1866) and *The Brothers Karamazov* (1880), as well as his journalism, including *A Writer's Diary*, completed during his last decade.

Rosamund Bartlett is a writer, scholar and translator. The author of biographies of Tolstoy and Chekhov, she has also published books on Wagner, Shostakovich and the Futurist opera *Victory Over The Sun*. Her new translation of *Anna Karenina* was published in 2014, and follows two anthologies of Chekhov stories and a volume of his letters. She has written on Russian literature, art and music for the *Financial Times*, the *Wall Street Journal*, *Apollo*, and the Royal Opera House, and worked with institutions such as the National Theatre, the Salzburg Festival and the Art Gallery of New South Wales in Sydney.

Fyodor Mikhailovich Dostoevsky

–

THE RUSSIAN SOUL

Selections from *A Writer's Diary*

–

introduced by
Rosamund Bartlett

Notting Hill Editions

Published in 2017 by Notting Hill Editions Ltd
Widworthy Barton Honiton Devon EX14 9JS

Designed by FLOK Design, Berlin, Germany
Typeset by CB editions, London

Printed and bound
by Memminger MedienCentrum, Memmingen, Germany

'Environment'; 'The Boy with His Hand Out'; 'The Boy at Christ's
Christmas Party'; 'The Peasant Marey'; ' My Paradox'; 'The Death of
George Sand'; 'A Few Words About George Sand': selected from 'A
Writer's Diary' Volume One, translated by Kenneth Lantz. Evanston:
Northwestern University Press, 1994. 'The Boy Celebrating His Saint's
Day'; 'Anna Karenina as a Fact of Special Importance'; 'A Lie Is Saved
by a Lie'; 'Pushkin (A Sketch)': selected from 'A Writer's Diary' Volume
Two, translated by Kenneth Lantz. Evanston: Northwestern University
Press, 1994. Copyright © 1994 Northwestern University Press.
Published 1994. All rights reserved.
'A Dream of a Ridiculous Man' translated by Olga Shartse.
Cover quote taken from 'Something about Lying', selected from 'A
Writer's Diary' Volume One, translated by Kenneth Lantz. Evanston:
Northwestern University Press, 1994.

Introduction copyright © 2017 by Rosamund Bartlett

The right of Rosamund Bartlett to be identified as the author of the
Introduction to this work has been asserted in accordance with Section
77 of the Copyright, Designs and Patents Act 1998

Series Editor: Johanna Möhring

Frontispiece: Fyodor Dostoevsky, copyright ITAR-TASS Photo Agency/
Alamy Stock Photo

A CIP record for this book is available from the British Library

ISBN 978-1-910749-63-0

www.nottinghilleditions.com

'. . . what truly matters here is that the Russian instinct has not died: the Russian soul, albeit unconsciously, has protested precisely in the name of its Russianness, in the name of its downtrodden and Russian principle.'

– Fyodor Dostoevsky, 'My Paradox', June 1876

Contents

Rosamund Bartlett

– Introduction –

Virulent nationalism, religious extremism, ethnic intolerance, urban deprivation, child abuse, suicide, opinionated criticism, intimate confession, utopian dreaming, genial digression, moral fervour, profound insight, macabre humour and superlative fiction – welcome to the world of Dostoevsky's *A Writer's Diary*. A voluminous and variegated miscellany in which the celebrated author spoke to his readers about issues concerning Russia, mostly directly, but sometimes indirectly via short stories, it is a work as eerily prescient of global preoccupations in the twenty-first century as it is frequently overlooked. Dostoevsky's *Writer's Diary* was also his creative laboratory. And as a work in which he was ultimately concerned with defining the elusive 'Russian soul', which he believed was most perfectly embodied by his forebear Pushkin, it is a source of fundamental importance in understanding the complex mind behind his artistic works.

A unique journalistic enterprise incorporating art and politics, and both non-fiction and fiction, in which Dostoevsky came to perform the roles of sole writer, editor and publisher, *A Writer's Diary* is his most original work. And he was adamant that his *Diary* be regarded as a single oeuvre, on a par with his novels, despite the somewhat piecemeal nature of its publication in monthly instalments over the course of what proved to be the last decade of his life. *A Writer's Diary* was also Dostoevsky's favourite work, but it has perennially remained in the shadow of his novels, in both its Russian and anglophone versions, despite the publication in 1994 of a comprehensive and authoritative English edition, from which all but one of the extracts anthologised here are drawn. One of the main reasons for the *Diary*'s relative obscurity is its sheer size: with a total number of pages equivalent to two of his novels put together, it is Dostoevsky's longest literary work. Also slightly daunting is the oddity of its hybrid contents, whose genre – which could be portrayed as a quixotic, probing, perhaps quintessentially Russian take on the essay – Dostoevsky purposefully made hard to categorise. Dostoevsky's position as a reactionary and ideologically problematic figure after the Revolution did not help. Despite the enormous popularity of *A Writer's Diary* during Dostoevsky's lifetime, it was only ever re-published once during the Soviet period, in 1929, just before Stalin's Cultural Revolution began placing strictures on the arts. Remarkably, it was not until 2011 that the first properly annotated complete edition was published in Russia (densely printed on fifteen hundred pages).

In the West, scholarship on *A Writer's Diary* was hampered for decades by an understandable reluctance to confront head-on the chauvinist and anti-semitic sentiments Dostoevsky expressed on its pages. By drawing a distinction between his artistic and political writings which their author never had, and mostly passing in silence over the latter, Western scholars were not able to investigate *A Writer's Diary* as a whole. That situation ended once and for all with the publication of the final volume of Joseph Frank's magisterial biography in 2002, and the flurry of books and articles which one can now consult about *A Writer's Diary*, by both Western and Russian scholars, suggests an eagerness to make up for lost time, and a re-assessment of the work's position in Dostoevsky's legacy. This anthology from *A Writer's Diary* brings together a representative selection of entries chosen to reflect the diverse nature of its contents. In them Dostoevsky demonstrates his great power as a writer, as well as his unerring ability to impart a deeper moral and religious resonance to the social and political concerns he raises.

When Dostoevsky began work on his *Writer's Diary* in 1873, he was fifty two years old, happily married, and an esteemed and established novelist. Such security had come at considerable personal cost, however, as we know from the traumatic facts of his earlier biography. The second son of an impecunious Moscow army doctor whose dutiful state service had brought him into the lower echelons of the noble class, the young Fyodor Dostoevsky set his heart on becoming a writer while studying at the Military

Engineering College in St Petersburg. He launched his literary career in 1843, the year of his graduation, with a translation of Balzac's then recent novel *Eugénie Grandet*. But it was not until two years later, having resigned his engineering lieutenant's commission, that he made his own debut. Shepherded by the influential progressive critic Vissarion Belinsky, the publication of *Poor Folk* brought him instantly into the front ranks of Russian writers. Dostoevsky's refusal to continue with that work's humanitarian theme in *The Double*, published in 1846, coupled with an inability to moderate his highly strung temperament, led to his equally swift fall from grace. But social ostracism within the small confines of St Petersburg's stiflingly small literary community was nothing compared to the Siberian exile which followed his arrest in April 1849 by the Secret Police.

Prodigiously well-read in the literature and thought of Romanticism, with a deep moral opposition to serfdom, Dostoevsky had naturally been drawn into the orbit of the Petrashevsky Circle, and the Charles Fourier-inspired discussions of French Utopian Socialism its members conducted behind closed doors. When these discussions became more heated as the 1848 Revolutions broke out across Europe, the paranoid Nicholas I took extreme action, determined to stamp out subversive activity in Russia at any cost. After enduring eight months of imprisonment in the notorious dungeon of the Peter and Paul

Fortress, Dostoevsky found himself being led to the stake and enduring a mock execution by firing squad before learning that his sentence was being commuted to hard labour in Siberia.

Four years of living in close confines with hardened criminals from the peasant class were followed by a further six serving as an army private and then officer in remote Semipalatinsk in what today would be Kazakhstan. But perhaps the hardest punishment of all for Dostoevsky to bear was his ten-year exile from the world of writing and publishing. And it was a world which had changed utterly by the time he was allowed to return to European Russia in 1859. Alexander II, the new Tsar on the throne, had been goaded by the catastrophe of the Crimean War into launching a programme of unprecedented reform, including the abolition of serfdom and the relaxation of censorship. But this would not satisfy the rational-minded new generation of the St Petersburg intelligentsia. Having jettisoned the comparatively gentle Utopian Socialism-imbued-with-Christianity of the 1840s as their guiding idea, in favour of Ludwig Feuerbach's atheist humanism and the Utilitarianism of Jeremy Bentham and John Stuart Mill, they wanted radical action. Dostoevsky, who had also changed during his years as a convict, and was now orientated towards a politically conservative, Christian ideal, was horrified. The publication of his novella *Notes from Underground* in 1864 marks the beginning of a new phase in his career as a writer. Dostoevsky's quest to engage creatively with the corrupting effects of the new ideologies from Western Europe, that he perceived were contaminating Russian youth, would lead to the writing of *Crime and Punishment*, *The Idiot* and *The Devils*, and culminate with his last novel *The Brothers Karamazov* in 1881. His *Writer's Diary* was part of this spiritual crusade. Dostoevsky wanted to show a different way forward for Russia, one that was rooted in the Christian values of the Russian Orthodox Church.

Dostoevsky's immediate impulse for embarking on *A Writer's Diary* was a desire to come into closer contact with his readers. By 1862 his reputation was secured with the publication of his semi-autobiography *Notes from the House of the Dead*, the first fiction to deal with the realities of Russia's penal system in Siberia. But there were further vicissitudes for him to contend with, including epilepsy, family mortalities, punitive publishing contracts and the constant and humiliating threat of destitution. A journal he optimistically set up with his brother Mikhail in 1861 was closed down in 1863, and its replacement foundered after Mikhail's death a year later, leaving him with heavy debts. These were soon compounded by losses from the pathological addiction to gambling Dostoevsky acquired during his visits abroad, and it was in order to escape his creditors that he remained in Western Europe from 1867 until 1871 with his second wife Anna Snitkina. He had plenty of ideas for fiction that he still wanted to explore after completing *The Devils*, but at the end of 1872, fearing that he had become cut off from the 'living stream' of life during his four years away from Russia, he agreed to become editor of a conservative weekly journal called *The Citizen*. He was pilloried for this by the liberal intelligentsia, but the job gave him a regular income for the first time in his life. Perhaps more crucially, it also gave him the opportunity to begin publishing in *The Citizen* a series of his musings about art and society without financial risk. The sixteen columns which Dostoevsky published irregularly over the course of 1873 under the title *A Writer's Diary* were thus a kind of trial balloon. As well as enabling him to reacquaint himself with Russian reality, they brought him back squarely into the public eye.

Unlike his contemporaries and main literary rivals Tolstoy and Turgenev, Dostoevsky was one of Russia's first professional authors, and relied on the income from his writing. He had not published an article in many years when he embarked on his *Writer's Diary*, but he was a seasoned journalist who had begun contributing to periodicals at the very beginning of his career. He was also successful: the journal he founded with his brother was the most popular new periodical of its day before its unfortunate and precipitous demise. Ever since those days, the creation of a personal almanac had been his long-held dream, and his choice of the *feuilleton* (the non-political, arts section of a newspaper) to be the main medium for his diary

entries was a considered one. The *feuilleton* was a popular genre dating from the 1840s that he himself had
deployed as a journalist. In it, a writer would range in a
sometimes random and whimsical manner over diverse
topics, from reviews to anecdotes, in the space of one
article. Its discursive style was a deliberate ploy, as was
its conversational and informal tone, and it was a perfect choice for Dostoevsky, as it gave him the freedom
to experiment with form. His political sympathies may
now have been conservative, but artistically he was still
a radical. Through the creation of a distinct authorial
persona, he could jump or meander from one subject
to another in his *Diary*, and, more daringly, switch
from non-fiction to fiction without preamble, remov-
ing any distinction between fact-based journalism and
artistic fantasy. The short stories embedded in the text
of the *Writer's Diary* stand on their own as independent works of art, but they can also be seen as parables,
serving as artistic illustrations of the ideological argu-
ments Dostoevsky puts forward in the articles which
surround them.

Like a good feuilletonist, Dostoevsky immediately
struck a confessional and improvisatory tone with
his reader in the first column of his *Writer's Diary*, in
which he voiced his uncertainty as to the direction this
new work would take:

What shall I talk about? About everything that strikes me and
sets me to thinking. And if I should find a reader and, God

forbid, an opponent, I realize that one must be able to carry on a conversation and know whom to address and how to address him. I shall try to master this skill because among us, that is to say, in literature, it is the most difficult one of all.

It was in his substantial and confident third column, entitled 'Environment', that Dostoevsky really began to get into his stride, polemicising with imaginary opponents, and presenting opposing views in a manner reminiscent of the great Socratic dialogues sustained in his novels. This was his method of hammering out his ideological stance, although in this particular case he had no real doubts, as the subject of 'Environment' was one that had been close to his heart ever since his time in Siberia when he had been a political prisoner shackled in irons. This was the problem of crime and punishment.

Amongst the sweeping judicial reforms introduced by Alexander II in the 1860s, the implementation of trial by jury was one of the most important, and Dostoevsky had spent long hours in the reading rooms of foreign libraries while he was abroad, avidly following court cases. Now that he had returned to St Petersburg, he could attend trials in person, and his *Writer's Diary* provided him with the perfect forum in which to report and comment on their proceedings. He was particularly exercised by the prevalence of acquittals secured by artful lawyers drawing on fashionable utilitarian theories about social determinism. In

'Environment', he related the case of a man who had beaten and abused his wife for so long she had finally hanged herself, yet he was still granted clemency. In Dostoevsky's hands, this was no dry narration of gruesome events, but a dramatic and heart-rending re-telling in which he let his creative imagination off the leash. The notion that environment could be posited as a legitimate defence in court cases was reprehensible to Dostoevsky, because it was tantamount to the removal of free choice and criminal responsibility, and he was uniquely qualified to speak out. The convicts he had encountered in prison, he pointed out, never ceased to regard themselves as criminals. As we know from Dostoevsky's major fiction, individual moral respon-sibility is one of his central themes. In *The Brothers Karamazov* he would extend it still further, arguing through his character of the Elder Zosima that no sin is in fact isolated, and that we are all responsible for everyone and everything.

Dostoevsky's *Writer's Diary* columns in 1873 were well received, but his duties at *The Citizen*, which included penning regular articles on foreign affairs, proved so onerous that he decided to relinquish his post as editor at the end of the year. Two years later, after the completion of his next novel, *A Raw Youth*, he was ready to devote himself again to his unusual journalistic project, and to take a gamble by publish-ing it himself, with the invaluable practical assistance of his wife. From 1876 until the end of 1877, the *Diary* appeared as an independent monthly journal, with each issue divided first into chapters, like a novel, and then into idiosyncratically titled sub-divisions. Every issue was continuously numbered, signed with Dostoevsky's name, then bound into a book at the end of the year to be sold as a separate volume, thus reinforcing the *Diary*'s overarching unity. Nothing like it had ever been published before in the history of Russian journalism. Although Dostoevsky was now limited to sixteen pages per issue, which, as an ex-convict, he had first to submit to the censor, it is telling that he nevertheless chose a large typeface. It was not just that he wanted to communicate his message to a wide audience, but that he wanted to break down the traditional barriers between the writer and the reader, liberate the printed word from conventions, and make it as intimate and oral as possible. Igor Volgin, Russia's leading Dostoevsky scholar, has gone so far to suggest that this quest to eradicate the modern disease of alienation amounted to a desire to restore human communication to a pre-Gutenberg state. Dostoevsky took pains now to write as if he was addressing a friend, using language that was simple and unaffected.

The contents of *A Writer's Diary* also changed once Dostoevsky became his own editor and publisher. He continued with the same mixture of journalism, memoir and commentary, seasoned with the occasional short story, but was no longer merely impelled to reveal the incompatibility of Christianity and Socialism, or the gulf between the corrupt educated class and the people. Dostoevsky's main focus now was to articulate and document the spiritual crisis he perceived in society. The collapse of moral and social foundations was attributable in his view to 'dissociation', which he understood biblically in terms of the original sin of separation from God, and whose most chilling expression was suicide. *A Writer's Diary* is full of suicides, as in the second chapter of his diary entry from January 1877, 'The Boy Celebrating his Saint's Day', for example. Dostoevsky moves from recounting an incident from Tolstoy's first piece of published fiction, *Childhood*, in which the young narrator dreams of killing himself after a minor misdemeanour, to discussion of a letter a reader had sent to him about the shocking real-life incident of a twelve-year-old boy who really had committed suicide. As a scion of the nobility, Tolstoy's hero could safely dream, Dostoevsky points out, 'while the other child dreamed it, and then he did it'. He was convinced there was not only something deeply wrong about the current epidemic of suicides, particularly those of children, but also about how little of Russian life had been properly observed by writers except that of the gentry, which he dismissed as insignificant and untypical. An element of missionary zeal can be detected in his rhetorical question as to who would be the 'historian' of all the other corners of Russian life, able to discern the essential principles surviving the ever-encroaching disintegration and chaos. This was Dostoevsky's mission in *A Writer's Diary*, also to predict the imminent arrival in Europe of a transcendent new era of Christian brotherly love and harmony inspired by the Russian people.

Since Dostoevsky was the devoted father of three young children in the 1870s, it is perhaps not surprising that broken-down, 'accidental' families emerge as a recurring leitmotif in his analysis of a society in crisis in *A Writer's Diary*. The suffering of children was probably the topic he found the most agonising of all, because it was a sticking point in his relationship with the Orthodox Church. There is a connection here with 'At Tikhon's', the controversial chapter of his recently completed novel *The Devils* that was considered too obscene to print in his lifetime. In it, the mysterious Nikolai Stavrogin presents Bishop Tikhon with his written confession of raping a twelve-year-old girl, and standing by passively when she subsequently hangs herself. Are there some sins for which one cannot be redeemed? Can one subscribe to a faith which allows the suffering of children? These questions, which would take centre stage in *The Brothers Karamazov*, are asked *sotto voce* throughout *A Writer's Diary* and are raised in the very first issue in its new imprint. Dostoevsky devotes part of the first chapter for January 1876 to describing the popular children's party hosted by the Artists' Club in St Petersburg where he had taken his daughter to see the Christmas tree. The first part of Chapter Two, 'The Boy with his Hand Out', contains Dostoevsky's sombre meditation on the dismal fate of poverty-stricken children from 'accidental families'. It was prompted by his repeated encounter in the days running up to Christmas with the same small, under-dressed boy begging on the streets in freezing conditions, and the discovery that there were 'hordes' of urchins like him enduring a similar existence. Dostoevsky then moves seamlessly in the second part of the chapter to 'The Boy at Christ's Christmas Party', his own made-up story about a newly orphaned urchin, six years old or younger, who dreams of being taken to heaven just as he in fact is perishing from the cold, alone in a courtyard.

In February 1876, Dostoevsky published a very special story about a suffering child which exemplifies the unifying idea of *A Writer's Diary*, and provides the missing link in the story of his religious conversion in Siberia. As he explains, he had invented a narrator for his *Notes from the House of the Dead*, and had hardly ever before spoken of his prison life in print. In 'The Peasant Marey', he recalls the disgust he had experienced in observing the drunken carousals of peasant convicts one Easter, and how it had led him to recall a moment in his own childhood when one of the family's serfs showed him kindness. The memory was a transformative and ecstatic experience, causing Dostoevsky to see Christian virtues not only in his fellow convicts, albeit heavily obscured by years of oppression, but in the Russian people as a whole. For Dostoevsky, the

Russian people preserved the Christian ideal at heart even while sinning, and therefore would play a pivotal role in the future salvation of Russia. Their supposed tendency towards extreme humility, need for suffering, and thirst for redemption are all ideas we meet in his fiction.

Children also feature prominently in the coverage of the many court cases in the new phase of *A Writer's Diary*. For Dostoevsky, trials reflected society's moral health, and so were the ideal grist to his mill. In 1873 he had briefly described examples of wife-beating and child abuse, but now he delved much deeper, in one spectacular case becoming personally involved, and influencing the course of justice. After briefly reporting in May 1876 on the crime of a peasant woman Ekaterina Kornilova, who had thrown her six-year-old step-daughter from an upstairs window, Dostoevsky wrote at length about her case that October. By then Kornilova had been sentenced to hard labour and permanent exile in Siberia, despite having turned herself in, and the child surviving unharmed. After writing about how his view of her conviction had been transformed by the discovery that she had been pregnant, Dostoevsky visited her in prison, and published the results of his psychological analysis in the December issue of his *Writer's Diary*. The following April, he was able to report that Kornilova had been acquitted.

Utterly at odds with the chapters in *A Writer's Diary* in which Dostoevsky writes with tenderness and compassion about children and miscarriages of justice, are those in which he talks, equally passionately, about politics. A new theme in the *Diary* appeared in June 1876 as war broke out in the Balkans. An upsurge of Pan-Slavist feeling led to advocacies of the unification of all Slavic peoples under Russian stewardship. This was Dostoevsky's vision of Russia's historic destiny. In a series of increasingly shrill and dogmatic articles published during the course of, first the Serbo-Turkish War from 1876 to 1878, and then the Russo-Turkish War from 1877 to 1878, he began to predict the displacement of the 'official Christianity' of the West by 'a true exaltation of the truth of Christ, which has been preserved in the East, a true, new exaltation of the cross of Christ and the ultimate word of Orthodoxy, at whose head Russia has long been standing'. Dostoevsky conceived Russia's involvement in the conflict in apocalyptic terms, defining it as a cataclysm like the French Revolution, from which a new world order would emerge. He not only took for granted Russia's claim to Constantinople, as undisputed leader of the Slav nations and protector of all Christians. His religious messianism also inspired megalomaniac dreams in which Russia's unique and superior Christian virtues would enable it to heal the rift between all the European nations at loggerheads over the longstanding 'Eastern Question'. This was the debate about how to react to the slowly collapsing Ottoman Empire, which threatened to undermine the ever-more fragile balance of power in Europe. A corollary of Dostoevsky's chauvinism was a deeply unpleasant xenophobia in which his greatest hostility was reserved for Russia's beleaguered Jewish population, most of whom were still confined to the reprehensible Pale of Settlement. This was the area established by Catherine the Great in 1791 while adding large swathes of territory to Imperial Russia's western borders during the Polish Partitions; the Empress forbade her new Jewish subjects from living outside the Pale, and even from residing in certain cities within it. The right to settle anywhere which was granted to Russia's wealthiest Jewish merchants in 1859 as part of Alexander II's reforms led to a policy of selective integration. The anti-Semitic theme began to surface in Dostoevsky's *Writer's Diary* in June 1876, along with the spectre of politics, and was soon keeping pace with his utopian nationalism, as expressed in his piece 'My Paradox'. Dostoevsky's vociferous tirades against Jewish people, whom he accused of profiteering from Russia's post-reform industrialisation boom, fill by far the most rebarbative pages in *A Writer's Diary*. They are all the more chilling for being expressions of his deeply held personal beliefs.

A few dissenting readers raised their heads over the parapet, but for the most part Dostoevsky's *Writer's Diary* was rapturously received and immediately became a best-seller, giving even the most popular journals of the time a run for their money. Some issues even had to be reprinted, and sales certainly far outstripped those for Dostoevsky's novels. He became a household name in Russia, even at the Imperial Court – an effusive letter was penned to the future Alexander III, who became a reader at the suggestion of Konstantin Pobedonostsev, Chief Procurator of the Holy Synod. The success of *A Writer's Diary* in its new incarnation marked a new and significant stage in Dostoevsky's career, in which he now assumed the role of moral teacher and prophet. If previously he wrote for and had been read by the small circles of the St Petersburg and Moscow intelligentsia, he was read now nationwide, by readers both young and old, representing all shades of the political spectrum. Feeling that he was the first writer to pay attention to ordinary Russians and was speaking directly to them, increasing numbers of readers also started sending Dostoevsky passionate letters from the furthest reaches of the provinces. Thus was his dream of entering into conversation with his readers about the issues he raised fulfilled. Correspondents who sought to take issue with his tendentious views ran the risk of their letters being picked apart in future issues of *A Writer's Diary*, but the majority responded warmly to his sincere and straightforward manner, if not with adulation and devotion. This kind of public engagement may not seem remarkable in an era in which readers are able to respond to articles online, but it was unprecedented in the history of Russian letters, and foreshadows the kinds of conversations which now take place on the internet. As such, Dostoevsky appears, in effect, as a blogger *avant la lettre*.

While Dostoevsky's verbose political harangues make for uncomfortable reading in his *Writer's Diary*, the many chapters in which he enters into a dialogue with fellow writers, past and present, or inserts his own pieces of short fiction, make the opposite impression, and remind us why we continue to regard him as one of the greatest literary figures of his age. In June 1876, shortly before launching into his reasons for distinguishing Russia from other European nations, he wrote a glowing obituary of George Sand, and about her supreme importance to his idealistic generation in the 1840s. In the subsequent, typically subjective piece he wrote about Sand, however, in which he assessed her legacy, it is interesting to note that he ascribed her socialist impulse to her innate moral sense. It had been Sand's 1837 novel *Mauprat*, set before the French Revolution, which had converted the influential Belinsky to French Utopian Socialism, from whose political ideology Dostoevsky clearly wished to disassociate himself now.

Of all the contemporary literary works with which Dostoevsky engaged on the pages of his *Writer's Diary*, Tolstoy's novel *Anna Karenina* was the most significant. The two great novelists had met on the page (*War and Peace* and *Crime and Punishment* were published simultaneously in the same journal, *The Russian Messenger*), but never in person. Supremely different beings in nearly every respect, they had hitherto been outwardly respectful, but wary of each other. When instalments of *Anna Karenina* started appearing in 1875, however, Dostoevsky could hardly ignore it in his *Writer's Diary*. To begin with, he was generous with his praise, particularly of Levin as a literary character, and devoted several pages to the novel in the February 1877 issue of his *Writer's Diary*. But when he read its conclusion later in the year, he was incensed, and in the July–August issue he lambasted Levin for being egocentric, unpatriotic and out of touch with the Russian people. Dostoevsky naturally took issue with Levin's claim that the Russian people shared his lack of concern for the predicament of the Balkan Slavs, and he also took exception to his declared unwillingness to kill, even if it resulted in the prevention of atrocities. People like Tolstoy were supposed to be our teachers, Dostoevsky thundered, but what exactly were they teaching us? Unlike Dostoevsky, of course, Tolstoy had seen active service. But Dostoevsky had lived in far greater proximity to the Russian people whom both writers revered.

Between Dostoevsky's two verdicts in the *Diary* on *Anna Karenina*, he published 'The Dream of a Ridiculous Man', his last piece of short fiction. This tightly-wrought short story presents Dostoevsky's major themes in microcosm, directly anticipating their amplification in *The Brothers Karamazov*, his last and most complex masterpiece. The trajectory of its deceptively simple plot is a perfect distillation of the writer's art. As usual, Dostoevsky felt no need to alert his reader to the transition from one register to another, or make any distinction between journalism and fiction. Russia had just declared war on Turkey, and the story appeared as a chapter in the April 1877 issue of the *Writer's Diary*, sandwiched between enthusiastic warmongering and an announcement of Ekaterina Kornilova's acquittal. 'The Dream of a Ridiculous Man' could thus be construed as an oblique attempt to suggest a solution to the underlying problems which had led to these events, but the story is complex, and can be interpreted in many different ways, some of which completely contradict each other. Readers of Dostoevsky's novels are familiar with the idea of the 'double'. It is the name of his early novella, and also refers to his practice of thematically linking characters in his fiction. In this case there is a direct link to 'The Meek One', another short story in *A Writer's Diary* with a theme of suicide, which was published earlier in November 1876. Both works bear the sub-title 'A Fantastic Story'. 'The Meek One' is a parable of the perils of dissociation which ends bleakly with a suicide, while the ridiculous man begins by failing to commit suicide, and only experiences it in his dream. Upon waking he is transfigured by his imagined experience of being transported to a utopian paradise of brotherly love, and ultimately embraces life. The story is a kind of allegory of Dostoevsky's own experience of confrontation with death, followed by his rejection of the socialist utopia systems produced by rational thought, and subsequent redemption through religious faith. It is also, as Dostoevsky's biographer Joseph Frank has pointed out, a kind of Russian *Candide*, which emulates Voltaire's satire on the ideas of the Enlightenment. Perhaps this is why a 'Voltaire armchair' is deliberately mentioned as one of the ridiculous man's few possessions.

While there are many who see 'The Dream of a Ridiculous Man' as Dostoevsky's most convincing portrayal of religious transformation and moral regeneration, it has also been interpreted as a parody, and even as blasphemy. There is, after all, great potential for ambiguity. Is 'The Dream of a Ridiculous Man' a fantastic story due to its supernatural content, for example, or the improbability of its message? Is the ridiculous man still ridiculous at the story's end, or are we meant to understand that he is ridiculous in a different way, or maybe even not ridiculous at all? The story certainly appears to show a path leading from the corrosive powers of Western rationalism to the Slavophile ideal of 'sobornost', or spiritual community, except that it is as yet one that is untrod.

Perhaps the main point about the story, as with Dostoevsky's *Writer's Diary* as a whole, and all his mature fiction, is that an element of doubt always remains, but this doubt is the grit that forms the pearl. 'The Dream of a Ridiculous Man' succeeds as a work of art precisely because it projects a journey towards an ideal, rather than the ideal itself. Dostoevsky's thirst for religious faith was genuine, but his often agonising scepticism ensured there was always more than one voice speaking in his writing. Even when he seems to be at his most strident, there was always a dialogue at some level, as becomes clear from the remarkable entry in his *A Writer's Diary* about Don Quixote. 'A Lie is Saved by a Lie' was written at the time of the Third Battle of Plevna in the Balkans between the Ottoman and Russian Empires in today's Bulgaria, and published in the issue for September 1877. Its subject is the often heroic necessity for self-deception which all humans must engage in at times order to bridge the painful gap between reality and the ideal.

Amongst the literary heroes who people *A Writer's Diary*, Don Quixote is by far the most important. Cherished by Dostoevsky as the greatest exemplar in literature of a 'positively beautiful' figure, along with Dickens' Pickwick and Hugo's Valjean, Don Quixote was an inspiration behind his own search to create a beautiful character, an artistic equivalent to Christ. It had already produced Prince Myshkin in *The Idiot*, and would lead finally to Alyosha in *The Brothers Karamazov*. Don Quixote is beautiful, but he is also ridiculous. In Dostoevsky's mind social failure was not just a criterion for beauty, but often a pre-requisite for holiness. 'A Lie is Saved by a Lie' contains Dostoevsky's meditations on Cervantes' masterpiece, as well as an invented scene which is in keeping with Don Quixote's noble illusion about the beauty of Dulcinea (whose name itself is an allusion to illusion). Perhaps this was Dostoevsky's best way of saying in so many words that his grand prophesies about Russia, and the imminent arrival of a new era of Christian harmony and brotherly love were a similar delusion in the face of nagging doubts.

Dostoevsky had planned to continue with his *Writer's Diary* beyond 1877, but was thwarted by ill health and the demands of writing *The Brothers Karamazov*. A single issue of *A Writer's Diary* appeared for August 1880, and it was dominated by the Pushkin speech he had just given. The unveiling of the first statue of the poet in Russia had been celebrated by four days of public events culminating in Dostoevsky's speech, which was greeted by a thirty-minute ovation, and an ecstatic outpouring of emotion. Dostoevsky had set out to explore the character and destiny of Russia and the Russian people in his *Writer's Diary*, and this speech seemed to sum everything up. It had been Pushkin with his purely Russian heart, he argued, who had been the first to show how educated Russian society had become tragically detached from its native soil and elevated itself 'above the People'; only if it embraced 'the People's truth' could it be resurrected. Pushkin was also the first to have created in his literary works 'artistic types of Russian beauty' emanating from the 'People's truth', as exemplified by his character Tatyana in *Eugene Onegin*. And it was Pushkin's

Russian soul, the embodiment of brotherly love, which explained his universality, and concomitant ability to transcend other nations. After the publication of his Pushkin speech, Dostoevsky went back to *The Brothers Karamazov*. He was by now very sick with pulmonary emphysema, but he had every hope of continuing with the *Diary*, and was still correcting proofs on the eve of his death. Copies of its single final issue went on sale on 1 February 1881, which was the day of his funeral.

– Environment –
(1873)

I think that all jurors the whole world over, and our jurors in particular, must share a feeling of power (they have other feelings as well, of course); more precisely, they have a feeling of autocratic power. This can be an ugly feeling, at least when it dominates their other feelings. Even though it may not be obvious, even though it may be suppressed by a mass of other, nobler emotions, this sense of autocratic power must be a strong presence in the heart of every juror, even when he is most acutely aware of his civic duty. I suppose that this is somehow a product of the laws of nature themselves. And so, I recall how terribly curious I was, in one respect at least, when our new (just) courts were instituted. In my flights of fancy I saw trials where almost all the jurors might be peasants who only yesterday were serfs. The prosecutor and the defence lawyers would address them, trying to curry favour and divine their mood, while our good peasants would sit and keep their mouths shut: 'So that's how things are these days. If I feel like lettin' the fella off, I'll do it; and if not, it's Siberia for him.'

And yet the surprising thing now is that they do not convict the accused but acquit them consistently.

Of course, this is also an exercise, almost even an abuse of power, but in one direction, toward an extreme, a sentimental one, perhaps – one can't tell. But it is a general, almost preconceived tendency, just as if everyone had conspired. There can be no doubt how widespread this 'tendency' is. And the problem is that the mania for acquittal regardless of the circumstances has developed not only among peasants, yesterday's insulted and humiliated, but has seized all Russian jurors, even those from the uppermost classes such as noblemen and university professors. The universality of this tendency in itself presents a most curious topic for reflection and leads one to diverse and sometimes even strange surmises.

Not long ago one of our most influential newspapers briefly set forth, in a very modest and well-intentioned little article, the following hypothesis: perhaps our jurors, as people who suddenly, without rhyme or reason, sense the magnitude of the power that has been conferred upon them (simply out of the blue, as it were), and who for centuries have been oppressed and downtrodden – perhaps they are inclined to take any opportunity to spite authorities such as the prosecutor, just for the fun of it or, so to say, for the sake of contrast with the past. Not a bad hypothesis and also not without a certain playful spirit of its own; but, of course, it can't explain everything.

'We just feel sorry to wreck the life of another person; after all, he's a human being too. Russians are compassionate people' – such is the conclusion reached by others, as I've sometimes heard it expressed.

However, I have always thought that in England, for instance, the people are also compassionate; and even if they do not have the same softheartedness as we Russians, then at least they have a sense of humanity; they have an awareness and a keen sense of Christian duty to their neighbour, a sense which, perhaps, taken to a high degree, to a firm and independent conviction, may be even stronger than ours, when you take into account the level of education over there and their long tradition of independent thought. Over there, such power didn't just tumble down on them out of the blue, after all. Indeed, they themselves invented the very system of trial by jury; they borrowed it from no one, but affirmed it through centuries; they took it from life and didn't merely receive it as a gift.

Yet over there the juror understands from the very moment he takes his place in the courtroom that he is not only a sensitive individual with a tender heart but is first of all a citizen. He even thinks (correctly or not) that fulfilling his civic duty stands even higher than any private victory of the heart. Not very long ago there was a clamour throughout the kingdom when a jury acquitted one notorious thief. The hubbub all over the country proved that if sentences just like ours are possible over there, then all the same they happen rarely, as exceptions, and they quickly rouse public indignation. An English juror understands above all that in his hands rests the banner of all England; that he has already ceased to be a private individual and is obliged to represent the opinion of his country. The capacity to be a citizen is just that capacity to elevate oneself to the level of the opinion of the entire country. Oh, yes, there are 'compassionate' verdicts there, and the influence of the 'corrupting environment' (our favourite doctrine now, it seems) is taken into consideration. But this is done only up to a certain limit, as far as is tolerated by the common sense of the country and the level of its informed and Christian morality (and that level, it seems, is quite high). Nonetheless, very often the English juror grudgingly pronounces the guilty verdict, understanding first of all that his duty consists primarily in using that verdict to bear witness to all his fellow citizens that in old England (for which any one of them is prepared to shed his blood) vice is still called vice and villainy is still called villainy, and that the moral foundations of the country endure – firm, unchanged, standing as they stood before.

'Suppose we do assume,' I hear a voice saying, 'that your firm foundations (Christian ones, that is) endure and that in truth one must be a citizen above all, must hold up the banner, etc., etc., as you said. I won't challenge that for the time being. But where do you think we'll find such a citizen in Russia? Just consider our situation only a few years ago! Civic rights (and what rights!) have tumbled down on our citizen as if from a mountain. They've crushed him, and they're still only a burden to him, a real burden!'

'Of course, there's truth in what you say,' I answer the voice, a bit despondent, 'but still, the Russian People . . .'

'The Russian People? Please!' says another voice. 'We've just heard that the boon of citizenship has tumbled down from the mountain and crushed the People. Perhaps they not only feel that they've received so much power as a gift, but even sense that it was wasted on them because they got it for nothing and aren't yet worthy of it. Please note that this certainly doesn't mean that they really aren't worthy of the gift, and that it was unnecessary or premature to give it; quite the contrary: the People themselves, in their humble conscience, acknowledge that they are unworthy, and the People's humble, yet lofty, awareness of their own unworthiness is precisely the guarantee that they are worthy. And meanwhile the People, in their humility, are troubled. Who has peered into the innermost secret places of their hearts? Is there anyone among us who can claim truly to know the Russian People? No, it's not simply a matter here of compassion and softheartedness, as you, sir, said so scoffingly. It's that this power itself is frightful! We have been frightened by this dreadful power over human fate, over the fate of our brethren, and until we mature into our citizenship, we will show mercy. We show mercy out of fear. We sit as jurors and think, perhaps: 'Are we any better than the accused? We have money and are free from want, but were we to be in his position we might do even worse than he did – so we show mercy.' So maybe it's a good thing, this heartfelt mercy. Maybe it's a pledge of some sublime form of Christianity of the future which the world has not yet known!'

'That's a partly Slavophile voice,' I think to my-self. It's truly a comforting thought, but the conjecture about the People's humility before the power they have received gratis and that has been bestowed upon them, still 'unworthy' of it, is, of course, somewhat neater than the suggestion that they want to 'tease the pros-ecutor a bit,' although even the latter still appeals to me because of its realism (accepting it, of course, more as an individual case, which indeed is what its author intended). But still . . . this is what troubles me most of all: how is it that our People suddenly began to be so afraid of a little suffering? 'It's a painful thing,' they say, 'to convict a man.' And what of it? So take your pain away with you. The truth stands higher than your pain.

In fact, if we consider that we ourselves are some-times even worse than the criminal, we thereby also acknowledge that we are half to blame for his crime. If he has transgressed the law which the nation pre-scribed for him, then we ourselves are to blame that he now stands before us. If we were better, then he, too, would be better and would not now be standing here before us . . .

'And so now we ought to acquit him?'

No, quite the contrary: now is precisely the time we must tell the truth and call evil evil; in return, we must ourselves take on half the burden of the sentence. We will enter the courtroom with the thought that we, too, are guilty. This pain of the heart, which everyone so fears now and which we will take with us when we leave the court, will be punishment for us. If this pain is genuine and severe, then it will purge us and make us better. And when we have made ourselves better, we will also improve the environment and make it better. And this is the only way it can be made better. But to flee from our own pity and acquit everyone so as not to suffer ourselves – why, that's too easy. Doing that, we slowly and surely come to the conclusion that there are no crimes at all, and 'the environment is to blame' for everything. We inevitably reach the point where we consider crime even a duty, a noble protest against the environment. 'Since society is organized in such a vile fashion, one can't get along in it without protest and without crimes.' 'Since society is organized in such a vile fashion, one can only break out of it with a knife in hand.' So runs the doctrine of the environment, as opposed to Christianity which, fully recognizing the pressure of the environment and having proclaimed mercy for the sinner, still places a moral duty on the individual to struggle with the environment and marks the line where the environment ends and duty begins.

In making the individual responsible, Christianity

thereby acknowledges his freedom. In making the individual dependent on every flaw in the social structure, however, the doctrine of the environment reduces him to an absolute nonentity, exempts him totally from every personal moral duty and from all independence, reduces him to the lowest form of slavery imaginable. If that's so, then if a man wants some tobacco and has no money, he can kill another to get some tobacco. And why not? An educated man, who suffers more keenly than an uneducated one from unsatisfied needs, requires money to satisfy them. So why shouldn't he kill an uneducated man if he has no other way of getting money? Haven't you listened to the voices of the defence lawyers: 'Of course,' they say, 'the law has been violated; of course he committed a crime in killing this uneducated man. But, gentlemen of the jury, take into consideration that . . .' And so on. Why such views have almost been expressed already, and not only 'almost' . . .

'But you, however,' says someone's sarcastic voice, 'you seem to be charging the People with subscribing to the latest theory of the environment; but how on earth did they get that theory? Sometimes these jurors sitting there are all peasants, and every one of them considers it a mortal sin to eat meat during the fasts. You should have just accused them squarely of harbouring social tendencies.'

'Of course, you're right – what do they care about 'environment,' the peasants as a whole, that is?' I think to myself. 'But still, these ideas float about in the air; there is something pervasive about an idea . . .'

'Listen to that, now!' laughs the sarcastic voice.

'But what if our People are particularly inclined toward this theory of the environment, by their very nature, or by their Slavic inclinations, if you like? What if they are the best raw material in Europe for those who preach such a doctrine?'

The sarcastic voice guffaws even louder, but it's a bit forced.

No, this is still only a trick someone is pulling on the People, not a 'philosophy of the environment.' There's a mistake here, a fraud, and a very seductive fraud.

One can explain this fraud, using an example at least, as follows:

Let's grant that the People do call criminals 'unfortunates' and give them pennies and bread. What do they mean by doing that, and what have they meant over the course of perhaps some centuries? Is it Christian truth or the truth of the 'environment?' Here is precisely where we find the stumbling block and the place where the lever is concealed which the propagator of 'the environment' could seize upon to effect.

Some ideas exist that are unexpressed and unconscious but that simply are strongly felt; many such ideas are fused, as it were, with the human heart. They are present in the People generally, and in humanity taken as a whole. Only while these ideas lie unconscious in peasant life and are simply felt strongly and truly can the People live a vigorous 'living life.' The whole energy of the life of the People consists in the striving to bring these hidden ideas to light. The more obstinately the People cling to them, the less capable they are of betraying their instincts, the less inclined they are to yield to diverse and erroneous explanations of these ideas – the stronger, more steadfast, and happier they are. Among such ideas concealed within the Russian People – the ideas of the Russian People – is the notion of calling a crime a misfortune and the criminal an unfortunate.

This notion is purely Russian. It has not been observed among any European people. In the West it's proclaimed only by some philosophers and thinkers. But our People proclaimed it long before their philosophers and thinkers. It does not follow, however, that the People would never be led astray at least temporarily or superficially by some thinker's false interpretation of this idea. The ultimate interpretation and the last word will remain, undoubtedly, always the People's, *but in the short term* this might not be the case.

To put it briefly, when they use the word 'unfortunate,' the People are saying to the 'unfortunate' more or less as follows:

'You have sinned and are suffering, but we, too, are sinners. Had we been in your place we might have done even worse. Were we better than we are, perhaps you might not be in prison. With the retribution for your crime you have also taken on the burden for all our lawlessness. Pray for us, and we pray for you. But for now, unfortunate ones, accept these alms of ours; we give them that you might know we remember you and have not broken our ties with you as a brother.'

You must agree that there is nothing easier than to apply the doctrine of 'environment' to such a view: 'Society is vile, and therefore we too are vile; but we are rich, we are secure, and it is only by chance that we escaped encountering the things you did. And had we encountered them, we would have acted as you did. Who is to blame? The environment is to blame. And so there is only a faulty social structure, but there is no crime whatsoever.'

And the trick I spoke of earlier is the sophistry used to draw such conclusions.

No, the People do not deny there is crime, and they know that the criminal is guilty. The People know that they also share the guilt in every crime. But by accusing themselves, they prove that they do not believe in 'environment'; they believe, on the contrary, that the environment depends completely on them, on their unceasing repentance and quest for self-perfection. Energy, work, and struggle – these are the means through which the environment is improved. Only by work and struggle do we attain independence and a sense of our own dignity. 'Let us become better, and the environment will be better.' This is what the Russian People sense so strongly but do not express in their concealed idea of the criminal as an unfortunate.

Now imagine if the criminal himself, hearing from the People that he is an 'unfortunate,' should consider himself only an unfortunate and not a criminal. In that case the People will renounce such a false interpretation and call it a betrayal of the People's truth and faith.

I could offer some examples of this, but let us set them aside for the moment and say the following.

The criminal and the person planning to commit a crime are two different people, but they belong to the same category. What if the criminal, consciously preparing to commit a crime, says to himself: 'There is no crime!' Will the People still call him an 'unfortunate'?

Perhaps they would; in fact they certainly would. The People are compassionate, and there is no one more unfortunate than one who has even ceased to consider himself a criminal: he is an animal, a beast. And what of it if he does not even understand that he is an animal and has crippled his own conscience? He is only doubly unfortunate. Doubly unfortunate, but also doubly a criminal. The People will feel compassion for him but will not renounce their own truth. Never have the People, in calling a criminal an 'unfortunate,' ceased to regard him as a criminal! And there could be no greater misfortune for us than if the People agreed with the criminal and replied to him: 'No, you are not guilty, for there is no "crime"'!

Such is our faith – our common faith, I should like to say; it is the faith of all who have hopes and expectations. I should like to add two more things.

I was in prison and saw criminals, hardened criminals. I repeat: it was a hard school. Not one of them ceased to regard himself as a criminal. In appearance they were a terrible and a cruel lot. Only the stupid ones or newcomers would 'put on a show,' however, and the others made fun of them. For the most part they were a gloomy, pensive lot. No one discussed his own crimes. I never heard a protest of any kind. Even speaking aloud of one's crimes was not done. From time to time we would hear a defiant or bragging voice, and all the prisoners, as one man, would cut the upstart short. Talking about *that* was simply not acceptable. Yet I believe that perhaps not one of them escaped the long inner suffering that cleansed and strengthened him. I saw them lonely and pensive; I saw them in church praying before confession; I listened to their single, unexpected words and exclamations; I remember their faces. Oh, believe me, in his heart not one of them considered himself justified!

I would not like my words to be taken as harsh. Still, I will risk speaking my mind and say plainly: with strict punishment, prison, and hard labor you would have saved perhaps half of them. You would have eased their burden, not increased it. Purification through suffering is easier – easier, I say, than the lot you assign to many of them by wholesale acquittals in court.

— THE RUSSIAN SOUL —

You only plant cynicism in their hearts; you leave them with a seductive question and with contempt for you yourselves. You don't believe it? They have contempt for you and your courts and for the justice system of the whole country! Into their hearts you pour disbelief in the People's truth, in God's truth; you leave them confused . . . The criminal walks out of the court thinking: 'So that's how it is now; they've gone soft. They've gotten clever, it seems. Maybe they're afraid. So I can do the same thing again. It's clear enough: I was in such a hard pinch, I couldn't help stealing.'

And do you really think that when you let them all off as innocent or with a recommendation for mercy you are giving them the chance to reform? He'll reform, all right! Why should he worry? 'It looks like I didn't do anything wrong at all' – this is what he thinks *in the final analysis.* You yourselves put that notion in his head. The main thing is that faith in the law and in the People's truth is being shaken.

Not long ago I spent several years living abroad. When I left Russia the new courts were only in their infancy. How eagerly I would read in our newspapers there everything concerning the Russian courts. With real sorrow I also observed Russians living abroad and their children, who did not know their native language or who were forgetting it. It was clear to me that half of them, by the very nature of things, would eventually become expatriates. I always found it painful to think about that: so much vitality, so many of the best, perhaps, of our people, while we in Russia are so in need of good people! But sometimes as I left the reading room, by God, gentlemen, I became reconciled to the temporary emigration and emigrés in spite of myself. My heart ached. I would read in the newspaper of a wife who murdered her husband and who was acquitted. The crime is obvious and proven; she herself confesses. 'Not guilty.' A young man breaks open a strongbox and steals the money. 'I was in love,' he says, 'very much in love, and I needed money to buy things for my mistress.' 'Not guilty.' It would not be so terrible if these cases could be justified by compassion or pity; but truly I could not understand the reasons for the acquittal and I was bewildered. I came away with a troubled feeling, almost as if I had been personally insulted. In these bitter moments I would sometimes imagine Russia as a kind of quagmire or swamp on which someone had contrived to build a palace. The surface of the soil looks firm and smooth, but in reality it is like the surface of some son of jellied green-pea aspic, and once you step on it you slip down to the very abyss. I reproached myself for my faintheartedness; I was encouraged by the thought that, being far away, I might be mistaken and that I myself was the kind of temporary emigré I spoke of; that I could not see things at first hand nor hear clearly . . .

And now I have been home again for a long while.

'But come now – do they really feel pity?' That's

the question! Don't laugh because I put so much stress on it. At least pity provides some sort of explanation; at least it leads you out of the darkness, and without it we comprehend nothing and see only gloomy blackness inhabited by some madman.

A peasant beats his wife, inflicts injuries on her for many years, abuses her worse than his dog. In despair to the point of suicide and scarcely in her right mind, she goes to the village court. They send her away with an indifferent mumble: 'Learn to live together.' Can this be pity? These are the dull words of a drunkard who has just come to after a long spree, a man who is scarcely aware that you an standing in front of him, who stupidly and listlessly waves you away so you won't bother him; a man whose tongue doesn't work properly, who has nothing in his head but alcohol fumes and folly.

The woman's story, by the way, is well known and happened only recently. We read about it in all the newspapers and, perhaps, we still remember it. Plainly and simply, the wife who suffered from her husband's beatings hanged herself; the husband was tried and found deserving of mercy. But for a long time thereafter I fancied I could see all the circumstances of the case; I see them even now.

I kept imagining his figure: he was tall, the reports said, very thickset, powerful, fair-haired. I would add another touch: thinning hair. His body is white and bloated; his movements slow and solemn; his gaze is steady. He speaks little and rarely and drops his words like precious pearls, cherishing them above all else. Witnesses testified that he had a cruel nature: he would catch a chicken and hang it by its feet, head down, just for his own pleasure. This amused him – a most characteristic trait! For a number of years he had beaten his wife with anything that was at hand – ropes or sticks. He would take up a floorboard, thrust her feet into the gap, press the board down, and beat and beat her. I think he himself did not know why he was beating her; he just did it, probably from the same motives for which he hung the chicken. He sometimes also starved her, giving her no bread for three days. He would place the bread on a shelf, summon her, and say: 'Don't you care touch that bread. That's my bread.' And that's another remarkably characteristic trait! She and her ten-year-old child would go off begging to the neighbours: if they were given bread they would eat; if not, they went hungry. When he asked her to work she did everything with never a hesitation or a murmur, intimidated, until finally she became a virtual madwoman. I can imagine what she looked like: she must have been a very small woman, thin as a rail. It sometimes happens that very large, heavy-set men with white, bloated bodies marry very small, skinny women (they are even inclined to choose such, I've noticed), and it is so strange to watch them standing or walking together. It seems to me that if she had become pregnant by him in her final days it would have been an even more characteristic and essential finishing touch; otherwise the picture is somehow incomplete. Have you seen how a peasant beats his wife? I have. He begins with a rope or a strap. Peasant life is without aesthetic pleasures such as music, theaters, and magazines; it is natural that this void be filled with something. Once he has bound his wife or thrust her feet into an opening in the floorboards, our peasant would begin, probably methodically, indifferently, even sleepily; his blows are measured; he doesn't listen to her cries and her pleading; or rather, he does listen, and listens with delight – otherwise what satisfaction would there be in beating her? Do you know, gentlemen, people are born in various circumstances: can you not conceive that this woman, in other circumstances, might have been some Juliet or Beatrice from Shakespeare, or Gretchen from *Faust*? I'm not saying that she was – it would be absurd to claim that – but yet there could be the embryo of something very noble in her soul, something no worse, perhaps, than what could be found in a woman of noble birth: a loving, even lofty, heart; a character filled with a most original beauty. The very fact that she hesitated so long in taking her own life shows something so quiet, meek, patient, and affectionate about her. And so this same Beatrice or Gretchen is beaten and whipped like a dog! The blows rain down faster and faster, harder and harder – countless blows. He begins to grow heated and finds it to his taste. At last he grows wild, and his wildness pleases him. The animal cries of his victim intoxicate him like liquor: 'I'll wash your feet and drink the water,' cries Beatrice in an inhuman voice. But finally she grows quiet; she stops shrieking and only groans wildly, her breath catching constantly; and now the blows come ever faster and ever more furiously . . . Suddenly he throws down the strap; like a madman he seizes a stick or a branch, anything he can find, and shatters it with three final, terrible blows across her back – enough! He steps away, sits down at the table, heaves a sigh, and sets to drinking his kvass. A small girl, their daughter (and they did have a daughter!) trembles on the stove in the corner, trying to hide: she has heard her mother crying. He walks out of the hut. Toward dawn the mother would revive and get up, groaning and crying with every movement, and set off to milk the cow, fetch water, go to work.

And as he leaves he tells her in his slow, methodical, and serious voice: 'Don't you dare eat that bread. That's *my* bread.'

Toward the end he also liked hanging her by her feet as well, the same way he had hung the chicken. Probably he would hang her, step aside, and sit down to have his porridge. When he had finished his meal he would suddenly seize the strap again and set to work on the hanging woman. The little girl, all a-tremble and huddled on the stove, would steal a wild glance at her mother hanging by her heels and try to hide again.

The mother hanged herself on a May morning,

a bright spring day, probably. She had been seen the night before, beaten and completely crazed. Before her death she had also made a trip to the village court, and there it was that they mumbled to her, 'Learn to live together.'

When the rope tightened around the mother's neck and she was making her last strangled cries, the little girl called out from the corner: 'Mamma, why are you choking?' Then she cautiously approached her, called out to the hanging woman, gazed wildly at her. In the course of the morning she came out of her corner to look at the mother again, until the father finally returned.

And now we see him before the court – solemn, puffy-faced, closely following the proceedings. He denies everything. 'We never spoke a sharp word to each other,' he says, dropping a few of his words like precious pearls. The jury leaves, and after a 'brief deliberation' they bring in the verdict: 'Guilty, but with *recommendation for clemency.*'

Note that the girl testified against her father. She told everything and, they say, wrung tears from the spectators. Had it not been for the 'clemency' of the jury he would have been exiled to Siberia. But with 'clemency' he need spend only eight months in prison and then come home and ask that his daughter, who testified against him on behalf of her mother, be returned to him. Once again he will have someone to hang by the heels.

'A recommendation for clemency!' And this verdict was given in full cognizance of the facts. They knew what awaited the child. Clemency to whom, and for what? You feel as if you are in some sort of whirlwind that's caught you up and twists and turns you around.

Wait a moment, I'll tell you one more story.

Once, before the new courts were established (not long before, however), I read of this particular little incident in our newspapers: a mother was holding in her arms her baby of a year or fourteen months. Children of that age are teething; they are ailing and cry and suffer a good deal. It seems the mother lost patience with the baby; perhaps she was very busy, and here she had to carry this child and listen to its heart-rending cries. She got angry. But can such a small child be beaten for something like this? It's a pity to strike it, and what can it understand anyway? It's so helpless and can't do a thing for itself. And even if you do beat it, it won't stop crying. Its little tears will just keep pouring out and it will put its arms around you; or else it will start to kiss you and just go on crying. So she didn't beat the child. A samovar full of boiling water stood in the room. She put the child's little hand right under the tap and opened it. She held the child's hand under the boiling water for a good ten seconds.

That's a fact; I read it. But now imagine if this happened today and the woman was brought to trial. The jury goes out and, 'after a brief deliberation,' brings in the verdict: 'Recommendation for clemency.'

Well, imagine: I invite mothers, at least, to imagine it. And the defence lawyer, no doubt, would probably start twisting the facts:

'Gentlemen of the jury, this is not what one could call a humane act, but you must consider the case as a whole; you must take into account the circumstances, the environment. This woman is poor; she is the only person working in the household; she puts up with a lot. She had not even the means to hire a nurse for her child. It is only natural that at a moment when, filled with anger caused by the corroding environment, so to say, gentlemen, it is only natural that she should have put the child's hand under the samovar tap . . ., and so . . .'

Oh, of course I fully appreciate the value of the legal profession; it is an elevated calling and a universally respected one. But one cannot help sometimes looking at it from a particular point of view – a frivolous one, I agree – but involuntary nonetheless: what an unbearable job it must be at times, one thinks. The lawyer dodges, twists himself around like a snake, lies against his own conscience, against his own convictions, against all morality, against all humanity! No, truly, he earns his money.

'Come, come!' exclaims suddenly the sarcastic voice we heard before. 'Why this is all nonsense, nothing but a product of your imagination. A jury never brought in such a verdict. No lawyer ever contorted the facts like that. You made it all up.'

But the wife, hung by her heels like a chicken; the 'This is my bread, don't you dare eat it'; the girl trembling on the stove, listening for half an hour to her mother's cries; and 'Mamma, why are you choking?' – isn't that just the same as the hand under the boiling water? Why it's *almost* the same!

'Backwardness, ignorance, the environment – have some pity,' the peasant's lawyer insisted. Yet millions of them do exist and not all hang their wives by their heels! There ought to be some limit here On the other hand, take an educated person: suppose he hangs his wife by her heels? Enough contortions, gentlemen of the bar. Enough of your 'environment.'

– The Boy with His Hand Out –

(January 1876)

C hildren are a strange lot; I dream of them and see them in my fancies. In the days before Christmas and on Christmas Eve itself I kept meeting on a certain street corner a little urchin who could have been no more than seven. In the terrible cold he was wearing clothes more fit for summer, but he did have some sort of old rag wrapped around his neck, which meant that someone had dressed him before sending him out. He was wandering 'with hand out'; that's a technical term meaning to go begging, a term coined by such boys themselves. There are many like him; they hang about you, whining some well-rehearsed phrases. But this boy didn't whine; his speech was innocent and unpracticed and he looked trustingly into my eyes; obviously he was only beginning this profession. In answer to my questions he said that he had a sister who was out of work and ill. Perhaps that was true, but only later did I learn that there are hordes of these urchins: they are sent 'with hands out' even in the most terrible cold, and if they collect nothing, they probably can expect a beating. Once a boy has collected a few kopecks, he returns with red, numbed hands to some cellar where a band of 'dodgers' are drinking. These are people who, 'quitting

24

work at the factory on Saturday night, return to work no earlier than Wednesday evening.' In the cellars their hungry and beaten wives drink with them; their hungry babies cry here too. Vodka, filth, and depravity, but vodka above all. With the kopecks he has collected in hand, the urchin is at once sent to a tavern and he brings back more vodka. Sometimes, for the fun of it, they pour half a bottle into his mouth and roar with laughter when, his breath catching, he falls to the floor scarcely conscious: '. . . and pitilessly he poured and poured/The horrid vodka into my mouth . . .'

When he gets older he's quickly packed off to a factory somewhere, but he's forced once again to bring all that he earns back to the dodgers, and they drink it up. But even before they get factory jobs these children become fully fledged criminals. They roam about the city and know places in various cellars into which they can crawl to spend the night unnoticed. One boy slept several nights in succession in a basket in the quarters of a janitor who never even noticed him. It is only natural that they become thieves. Thievery becomes a passion even among eight-year-olds, who sometimes even have no awareness of the criminality of their actions. In the end they bear it all – the hunger, cold, beatings – only for one thing, for freedom. And they run away from the dodgers to take up a vagrant's life on their own. A wild creature such as this sometimes knows nothing at all – neither where he lives, nor what nation he comes from; whether God exists, or the tsar.

There are even stories told about them that are hard to believe, yet they are facts.

– The Boy at Christ's Christmas Party –
(January 1876)

But I am a novelist and one 'story,' it seems, I made up myself. Why do I say 'it seems' when I know very well that I made it up? Yet I keep imagining that it really happened somewhere, sometime, and happened precisely on Christmas Eve in *a certain* huge city during a terrible cold spell.

I dreamed there was a boy – still very small, about six or even younger – who awoke one morning in the damp and cold cellar where he lived. He was wearing a wretched wrapper of some sort and he was trembling. His breath escaped in a white cloud and, while he sat, bored, in the corner on a trunk, he would let this white vapour out of his mouth and amuse himself by watching it billow up. But he was very hungry. Several times that morning he had approached the bed on which his sick mother lay on a mattress as thin as a pancake, a bundle beneath her head to serve as a pillow. How did she come to be here? Probably she had come with her boy from another city and suddenly fell ill. The landlady of this wretched tenement had been picked up by the police two days ago; the other tenants had all gone off, it being the holiday season, leaving but one dodger who had been lying in a drunken stupor for the last twenty-four hours, having been unable even to wait for the holiday. In another corner of the room an old woman of eighty groaned with rheumatism. She had once worked somewhere as a children's nurse but now was dying alone, moaning, grumbling, and complaining at the boy so that he had become frightened of approaching her corner. In the entry way he managed to find some water to quench his thirst, but nowhere could he find a crust of bread; again and again he went to wake his mother. At last he grew frightened in the darkness; the evening was well advanced, but still no candle had been lit. When he felt his mother's face he was surprised that she made no movement and had become as cold as the wall. 'And it's dreadful cold in here,' he thought. He stood for a time, absently resting his hand on the dead woman's shoulder; then he breathed on his fingers to warm them, and suddenly his wandering fingers felt his cap that lay on the bed; quietly he groped his way out of the cellar. He would have gone even before but he was afraid of the big dog that howled all day long by the neighbour's door on the stairway above. But the dog was no longer there, and in a thrice he was out on the street.

Heavens, what a city! He had never seen anything like it before. In the place he had come from there was such gloomy darkness at night, with only one lamppost for the whole street. The tiny wooden houses were closed in by shutters; as soon as it got dark you wouldn't see a soul on the street; everyone would lock themselves in their houses, only there would be huge packs of dogs – hundreds and thousands of dogs – howling and barking all night. Still, it was so nice and warm there, and there'd be something to eat; but here – Dear Lord, if only there was something to eat! And what a rattling and a thundering there was here, so much light, and so many people, horses, and carriages, and the cold – oh, the cold! Frozen vapor rolls from the overdriven horses and streams from their hot, panting muzzles; their horseshoes ring against the paving stones under the fluffy snow, and everyone's pushing each other, and, Oh Lord, I'm so hungry, even just a little bite of something, and all of a sudden my fingers are aching so. One of our guardians of the law passed by and averted his eyes so as not to notice the boy.

And here's another street – look how wide it is! I'll get run over here for sure. See how everyone's shouting and rushing and driving along, and the lights – just look at them! Now what can this be? What a big window, and in the room behind the glass there's a tree that stretches right up to the ceiling. It's a Christmas tree, with oh, so many lights on it, so many bits of gold paper and apples; and there's dolls and little toy horses all around it; children are running around the room, clean and dressed in nice clothes, laughing and playing, eating and drinking something. Look at that girl dancing with the boy, how fine she is! And you can even hear the music right through the glass. The little boy looks on in amazement and even laughs; but now his toes are aching and his fingers are quite red; he can't bend them any more, and it hurts when he tries to move them. The boy suddenly thought of how much his fingers hurt, and he burst into tears and ran off, and once more he sees a room through another window, and this one also has trees, but there are cakes on the tables, all sorts of cakes – almond ones, red ones, yellow ones; and four rich ladies are sitting there giving cakes to anyone who comes in. The door is always opening to let in all these fine people from the street. The boy crept up, quickly pushed open the door, and went in. Heavens, how they shouted at him and waved him away! One of the ladies rushed up to him and shoved a kopeck in his hand; then she opened the door to let him out on the street again. How frightened he was! And the kopeck rolled right out of his hand and bounced down the stairs; he couldn't bend his red fingers to hold on to it. The boy ran off as quickly as he could, but had no notion of where he was going. He felt like crying again, but he was afraid and just kept on running, breathing on his fingers. And his heart ached because suddenly he felt so lonely and so frightened, and then – Oh, Lord! What's happening now? There's a crowd of people standing around gaping at something: behind the glass in the window there are three puppets, little ones dressed up in red and green and looking just like they were alive! One of them's a little old man, sitting there like he's playing on a big violin, and the others are standing playing on tiny fiddles, wagging their heads in time to the music and looking at one another; their lips are moving and they're talking, really talking, only you can't hear them through the glass. At first the boy thought that they were alive, but when he finally realized that they were puppets he burst out laughing. He had never seen such puppets before and had no idea that such things existed! He still felt like crying, but it was so funny watching the puppets. Suddenly he felt someone grab him from behind: a big brute of a boy stood beside him and suddenly cracked him on the head, tore off his cap, and kicked at his legs. The boy fell down, and the people around him began shouting; he was struck with terror, jumped to his feet and ran off as fast as he could, wherever his legs would take him – through a gateway into a courtyard where he crouched down behind a pile of wood. 'They won't find me here, and it's good and dark as well.'

He sat there, cowering and unable to catch his breath from fear, and then, quite suddenly, he felt so good: his hands and feet at once stopped aching and he felt as warm and cozy as if he were next to the stove. Then a shudder passed over him: 'Why I almost fell asleep!' How nice it would be to go to sleep here: 'I'll sit here for a bit and then go back to have a look at those puppets,' he thought, and grinned as he recalled them. 'Just like they were alive! . . .' Then suddenly he heard his mother singing him a song as she bent over

31

him. 'Mamma, I'm going to sleep; oh, how nice it is to sleep here!'

Then a quiet voice whispered over him: 'Come with me, son, to my Christmas party.'

At first he thought that it was still his mamma, but no – it couldn't be. He couldn't see who had called him, but someone bent over him and hugged him in the darkness; he stretched out his hand . . . and suddenly – what a light there was! And what a Christmas tree! It was more than a tree – he had never seen anything like it! Where can he be? Everything sparkles and shines and there are dolls everywhere – but no, they are all girls and boys, only they are so radiant and they all fly around him, kissing him, picking him up and carrying him off; but he's flying himself; and he sees his mother looking at him and laughs joyously to her.

'Mamma! Mamma! How lovely it is here, mamma!' cries the boy; and he kisses the children again and wants at once to tell them about the puppets behind the glass. 'Who are you, boys and girls?' he asks, laughing and feeling that he loves them all.

'This is Christ's Christmas party,' they answer. 'On this day Christ always has a Christmas party for those little children who have no Christmas tree of their own . . .' And he learned that all these boys and girls were children just like him, but some had frozen to death in the baskets in which they had been abandoned on the doorsteps of Petersburg officials, others had perished in the keeping of indifferent nurses in orphans' homes,

still others had died at the dried-up breasts of their
mothers during the Samara famine, and yet others had
suffocated from the fumes in third-class railway carriages. And now they are all here, all like angels, all
with Christ; and He is in their midst, stretching out
His hands to them, blessing them and their sinful
mothers. And the mothers of the children stand apart,
weeping; each one recognizes her son or daughter; and
the children fly to their mothers and wipe away their
tears with their tiny hands, begging them not to weep
because they are so happy here . . .

Down below, the next morning, the porters found
the tiny body of the runaway boy who had frozen to
death behind the woodpile; they found his mother as
well . . . She had died even before him; they met in
God's Heaven.

So why did I make up a story like that, so little
in keeping with the usual spirit of a sober-minded diary, and a writer's diary at that? All the more since I
promised stories preeminently about actual events!
But that's just the point: I keep imagining that all this
could really have happened – I mean the things that
happened in the cellar and behind the woodpile; as
for Christ's Christmas party – well, I really don't know
what to say: could that have happened? That's just why
I'm a novelist – to invent things.

– The Peasant Marey –
(February 1876)

But reading all these *professions de foi*[1] is a bore, I think, and so I'll tell you a story; actually, it's not even a story, but only a reminiscence of something that happened long ago and that, for some reason, I would very much like to recount here and now, as a conclusion to our treatise on the People. At the time I was only nine years old. But no, I'd best begin with the time I was twenty-nine.

It was the second day of Easter Week. The air was warm, the sky was blue, the sun was high, warm, and bright, but there was only gloom in my heart. I was wandering behind the prison bar-racks, examining and counting off the pales in the sturdy prison stockade, but I had lost even the desire to count, although such was my habit. It was the second day of 'marking the holiday' within the prison compound; the prisoners were not taken out to work; many were drunk; there were shouts of abuse, and quarrels were constantly breaking out in all corners. Disgraceful, hideous songs; card games in little nooks under the bunks; a few convicts, already beaten half to death by sentence

1 Declarations of principles.

34

of their comrades for their particular rowdiness, lay on bunks covered with sheepskin coats until such time as they might come to their senses; knives had already been drawn a few times – all this, in two days of holiday, had worn me out to the point of illness. Indeed, I never could endure the drunken carousals of peasants without being disgusted, and here, in this place, particularly. During these days even the prison staff did not look in; they made no searches, nor did they check for alcohol, for they realized that once a year they had to allow even these outcasts to have a spree; otherwise it might be even worse. At last, anger welled up in my heart. I ran across the Pole M—cki, a political prisoner; he gave me a gloomy look, his eyes glittering and his lips trembling: 'Je hais ces brigands!'[2] he muttered, gritting his teeth, and passed me by. I returned to the barrack despite the fact that a quarter-hour before I had fled it half-demented when six healthy peasants had thrown themselves, as one man, on the drunken Tatar Gazin and had begun beating him to make him settle down; they beat him senselessly with such blows as might have killed a camel; but they knew that it was not easy to kill this Hercules and so they didn't hold back. And now when I returned to the barracks I noticed Gazin lying senseless on a bunk in the corner showing scarcely any signs of life; he was lying under a sheepskin coat, and everyone passed him by in silence:

2 'I hate these bandits!'

although they firmly hoped he would revive the next morning, still, 'with a beating like that, God forbid, you could finish a man off.' I made my way to my bunk opposite a window with an iron grating and lay down on my back, my hands behind my head, and closed my eyes. I liked to lie like that: a sleeping man was left alone, while at the same time one could daydream and think. But dreams did not come to me; my heart beat restlessly, and M—cki's words kept echoing in my ears: 'Je hais ces brigands!' However, why describe my feelings? Even now at night I sometimes dream of that time, and none of my dreams are more agonizing. Perhaps you will also notice that until today I have scarcely ever spoken in print of my prison life; I wrote *Notes from the House of the Dead* fifteen years ago using an invented narrator, a criminal who supposedly had murdered his wife. (I might add, by the way, that many people supposed and are even now quite firmly convinced that I was sent to hard labor for the murder of my wife.)

Little by little I lost myself in reverie and imperceptibly sank into memories of the past. All through my four years in prison I continually thought of all my past days, and I think I relived the whole of my former life in my memories. These memories arose in my mind of themselves; rarely did I summon them up consciously. They would begin from a certain point, some little thing that was often barely perceptible, and then bit by bit they would grow into a finished picture, some strong and complete impression. I would analyse these impressions, adding new touches to things experienced long ago; and the main thing was that I would refine them, continually refine them, and in this consisted my entire entertainment. This time, for some reason, I suddenly recalled a moment of no apparent significance from my early childhood when I was only nine years old, a moment that I thought I had completely forgotten; but at that time I was particularly fond of memories of my very early childhood. I recalled one August at our home in the country: the day was clear and dry, but a bit chilly and windy; summer was on the wane, and soon I would have to go back to Moscow to spend the whole winter in boredom over my French lessons; and I was so sorry to have to leave the country. I passed by the granaries, made my way down into the gully, and climbed up into the Dell – that was what we called a thick patch of bushes that stretched from the far side of the gully to a grove of trees. And so I make my way deeper into the bushes and can hear that some thirty paces away a solitary peasant is plowing in the clearing. I know he's plowing up the steep side of a hill and his horse finds it heavy going; from time to time I hear his shout, 'Gee-up!' I know almost all our peasants, but don't recognize the one who's plowing; and what difference does it make, anyway, since I'm quite absorbed in my own business. I also have an occupation: I'm breaking off a switch of walnut to lash frogs; walnut switches are so lovely and quite without flaws, so much better than birch ones. I'm also busy with bugs and beetles, collecting them; some are very pretty; I love the small, nimble, red-and-yellow lizards with the little black spots as well, but I'm afraid of snakes. I come across snakes far less often than lizards, however. There aren't many mushrooms here; you have to go into the birch wood for mushrooms, and that's what I have in mind. I liked nothing better than the forest with its mushrooms and wild berries, its insects, and its birds, hedgehogs, and squirrels, and with its damp aroma of rotting leaves that I loved so. And even now, as I write this, I can catch the fragrance from our stand of birches in the country: these impressions stay with you all your life. Suddenly, amid the deep silence, I clearly and distinctly heard a shout: 'There's a wolf!' I screamed, and, beside myself with terror, crying at the top of my voice, I ran out into the field, straight at the plowing peasant.

It was our peasant Marey. I don't know if there is such a name, but everyone called him Marey. He was a man of about fifty, heavy-set, rather tall, with heavy streaks of gray in his bushy, dark-brown beard. I knew him but had scarcely ever had occasion to speak to him before. He even stopped his little filly when he heard my cry, and when I rushed up to him and seized his plow with one hand and his sleeve with the other, he saw how terrified I was.

'It's a wolf!' I cried, completely out of breath.

Instinctively he jerked his head to look around, for an instant almost believing me.

'Where's the wolf?'

'I heard a shout . . . Someone just shouted, "Wolf"'
. . . I babbled.

'What do you mean, lad? There's no wolf; you're just hearing reassuring me. But I was all a-tremble and clung to his coat even more tightly; I suppose I was very pale as well. He looked at me with an uneasy smile, evidently concerned and alarmed for me.

'Why you took a real fright, you did!' he said, wagging his head. 'Never mind, now, my dear. What a fine lad you are!'

He stretched out his hand and suddenly stroked my cheek.

'Never mind, now, there's nothing to be afraid of. Christ be with you. Cross yourself, lad.' But I couldn't cross myself; the corners of my mouth were trembling, and I think this particularly struck him. He quietly stretched out a thick, earth-soiled finger with a black nail and gently touched it to my trembling lips.

'Now, now,' he smiled at me with a broad, almost maternal smile. 'Lord, what a dreadful fuss. Dear, dear, dear!'

At last I realized that there was no wolf and that I must have imagined hearing the cry of 'Wolf.' Still, it had been such a clear and distinct shout; two or three times before, however, I had imagined such cries (not only about wolves), and I was aware of that. (Later, when childhood passed, these hallucinations did as well.)

'Well, I'll be off now,' I said, making it seem like a question and looking at him shyly.

'Off with you, then, and I'll keep an eye on you as you go. Can't let the wolf get you!' he added, still giving me a maternal smile. 'Well, Christ be with you, off you go.' He made the sign of the cross over me, and crossed himself. I set off, looking over my shoulder almost every ten steps. Marey continued to stand with his little filly, looking after me and nodding every time I looked around. I confess I felt a little ashamed at taking such a fright. But I went on, still with a good deal of fear of the wolf, until I had gone up the slope of the gully to the first threshing barn; and here the fear vanished entirely, and suddenly our dog Volchok came dashing out to meet me. With Volchok I felt totally reassured, and I turned toward Marey for the last time; I could no longer make out his face clearly, but I felt that he was still smiling kindly at me and nodding. I waved to him, and he returned my wave and urged on his little filly.

'Gee-up,' came his distant shout once more, and his little filly once more started drawing the wooden plow.

This memory came to me all at once – I don't know why – but with amazing clarity of detail. Suddenly I roused myself and sat on the bunk; I recall that a quiet smile of reminiscence still played on my face. I kept on recollecting for yet another minute.

I remembered that when I had come home from

Marey I told no one about my 'adventure.' And what
kind of adventure was it anyway? I forgot about Marey
very quickly as well. On the rare occasions when I met
him later, I never struck up a conversation with him,
either about the wolf or anything else, and now, suddenly, twenty years later, in Siberia, I remembered that
encounter so vividly, right down to the last detail. That
means it had settled unnoticed in my heart, all by itself
with no will of mine, and had suddenly come back to
me at a time when it was needed; I recalled the tender,
maternal smile of a poor serf, the way he crossed me
and shook his head: 'Well you did take a fright now,
didn't you, lad!' And I especially remember his thick
finger, soiled with dirt, that he touched quietly and
with shy tenderness to my trembling lips. Of course,
anyone would try to reassure a child, but here in this
solitary encounter something quite different had happened, and had I been his very own son he could not
have looked at me with a glance that radiated more
pure love, and who had prompted him to do that? He
was our own serf, and I was his master's little boy; no
one would learn of his kindness to me and reward him
for it. Was he, maybe, especially fond of small children? There are such people. Our encounter was solitary, in an open field, and only God, perhaps, looking
down saw what deep and enlightened human feeling
and what delicate, almost feminine tenderness could
fill the heart of a coarse, bestially ignorant Russian
serf who at the time did not expect or even dream of

his freedom. Now tell me, is this not what Konstantin Aksakov had in mind when he spoke of the advanced level of development of our Russian People?

And so when I climbed down from my bunk and looked around, I remember I suddenly felt I could re-gard these unfortunates in an entirely different way and that suddenly, through some sort of miracle, the former hatred and anger in my heart had vanished. I went off, peering intently into the faces of those I met. This disgraced peasant, with shaven head and brands on his cheek, drunk and roaring out his hoarse, drunk-en song – why he might also be that very same Marey; I cannot peer into his heart, after all. That same evening I met M—cki once again. The unfortunate man! He had no recollections of any Mareys and no other view of these people but 'Je hais ces brigands!' No, the Poles had to bear more than we did in those days!

– The Death of George Sand –
(June 1876)

T he type for the May issue of the *Diary* had already been set, and it was being printed when I
read in the newspapers of the death of George Sand.
She died on May 27 (June 8 by the European calen-
dar), and so I was not able to say a word about her passing. And yet merely reading about her made me realize
what her name had meant in my life, how enraptured
I had been with this poet at one time, how devoted I
was to her, and how much delight and happiness she
once gave me! I write each of these words without
hesitation because they express quite literally the way
things were. She was entirely one of our (I mean *our*)
contemporaries – an idealist of the 1830s and 1840s.
In our mighty, self-important, yet unhealthy century,
filled with foggy ideals and impossible hopes, hers
is one of those names that emerged in Europe, 'the
land of sacred miracles,' and drew from us, from our
Russia which is forever creating itself, so many of our
thoughts, so much of our love, so much of the sacred
and noble force of our aspirations, our 'living life,' and
our cherished convictions. But we must not complain
about that: in exalting such names and paying them
homage, we Russians served and now serve our proper

mission. Do not be surprised at these words of mine, particularly when said about George Sand, who is still, perhaps, a controversial figure and whom half, if not nine-tenths of us, have already managed to forget; yet she still accomplished her task among us in days gone by. Who, then, should assemble around her grave to say a word in remembrance if not we, her contemporaries from all over the world? We Russians have two homelands: our own Russia and Europe, even if we call ourselves Slavophiles (and I hope the Slavophiles won't be angry at me for saying so). We need not dispute this point. The greatest of all the great missions that the Russians realize lies ahead of them is the common human mission; it is service to humanity as a whole, not merely to Russia, not merely to the Slavs, but to humanity as a whole. Think about it and you will agree that the Slavophiles recognized that very thing, and that is why they called on us to be more rigorous, more firm, and more responsible as Russians: they clearly understood that universality is the most important personal characteristic and purpose of the Russian. However, all this needs to be explained much more clearly: the fact is that service to the idea of universality is one thing, while traipsing frivolously around Europe after voluntarily and peevishly forsaking one's native land is something utterly opposed to it, yet people continue to confuse the two. No, this is not the case at all: many, very many of the things we took from Europe and transplanted in our own soil were not simply copied like slaves from their masters as the Potugins always insist we should; they were inoculated into our organism, into our very flesh and blood. There are some things, indeed, that we lived through and survived *independently*, just as they did there in the West, where such things were indigenous. The Europeans absolutely refuse to believe this: they do not know us, and for the moment this is all to the better. The essential process – which eventually will astonish the whole world – will take place all the more imperceptibly and peacefully. Part of that very process shows clearly and tangibly in our attitude toward the literatures of other peoples. For us – at least for the majority of our educated people – their poets are just as much ours as they are for the Europeans in the West. I maintain and I repeat: every European poet, thinker, and humanitarian is more clearly and more intimately understood and received in Russia than he is in any other country in the world save his own. Shakespeare, Byron, Walter Scott, and Dickens are more akin to the Russians and better understood by them than they are by the Germans, for example, despite the fact that we have not a tenth of the translations of these writers that Germany, with its abundance of books, has. When the French Convention of 1793 bestowed honorary citizenship *au poète allemand* Schiller, *l'ami de l'humanité*, it did something admirable, grand, and prophetic; yet it did not even suspect that at the other end of Europe, in barbaric Russia, that same Schiller was far more 'national' and far more familiar to the Russian barbarians than he was to France, not only the France of the time but subsequently as well, all through our century. This was an age in which Schiller, the citizen of France and *l'ami de l'humanité*, was known in France only by professors of literature, and not even known by all of them, and not known well. But he, along with Zhukovsky, was absorbed into the Russian soul; he left his mark on it and all but gave his name to a period in the history of our development. This Russian attitude to world literature is a phenomenon whose extent is scarcely found among other peoples anywhere in world history. And if this quality is truly our distinctively Russian national trait, then surely no oversensitive patriotism or chauvinism could have the right to object to it and not desire, on the contrary, to regard it primarily as a most promising and prophetic fact to be kept in mind as we speculate about our future. Oh, of course many of you may smile when you read of the significance I attribute to George Sand; but those who find it amusing will be wrong: a good deal of time separates us from those events, and George Sand herself has died as an old woman of seventy having, perhaps, long outlived her fame. But everything in the life of this poet that constituted the 'new word' she uttered, everything that was 'universally human' in her – all of this at once created a deep and powerful impression among us, in our Russia at the time. It touched us, and thus it proved that any poet and innovator from Europe, anyone who appears there with new ideas and new force, cannot help but become at once a Russian poet, cannot but influence Russian thought, cannot but become almost a Russian force. However, I do not mean to write a whole critical article about George Sand; I intended only to say a few words of farewell to the deceased by the side of her fresh grave.

– A Few Words about George Sand –
(June 1876)

George Sand appeared in literature when I was in my early youth, and I am very pleased that it was so long ago because now, more than thirty years later, I can speak almost with complete frankness. I should note that at the time her sort of thing – novels, I mean – was all that was permitted; all the rest, including virtually every new idea, and those coming from France in particular, was strictly suppressed. Oh, of course it often happened that they weren't able to pick out such 'ideas,' and indeed, where could they learn such a skill? Even Metternich lacked it, never mind those here who tried to imitate him. And so some 'shocking things' would slip through (the whole of Belinsky slipped through, for instance). And then, as if to make up for Belinsky (near the end of the period, in particular) and be on the safe side, they began to forbid almost everything so that, as we know, we were left with little more than pages with blank lines on them. But novels were still permitted at the beginning, the middle, and even at the very end of the period. It was here, and specifically with George Sand, that the public's guardians made a very large blunder. Do you remember the verse:

The tomes of Thiers and of Rabaut
He knows, each line by line;
And he, like furious Mirabeau
Hails Liberty divine.

These are very fine verses, exceptionally so, and they will last forever because they have historic significance; but they are all the more precious because they were written by Denis Davydov, the poet, literary figure, and most honorable Russian. But even if in those days Denis Davydov considered Thiers, of all people (on account of his history of the revolution, of course) as dangerous and put him in a verse along with some Rabaut fellow (such a man also existed, it seems, but I don't know him), then there surely could not have been much that was permitted officially then. And what was the result? The whole rush of new ideas that came through the novels of the time served exactly the same ends, and perhaps by the standards of the day in an even more 'dangerous' form, since there probably were not too many lovers of Rabaut, but there were thousands who loved George Sand. It should also be noted here that, despite all the Magnitskys and the Liprandis, ever since the eighteenth century people in Russia have at once learned about every intellectual movement in Europe, and these ideas have been at once passed down from the higher levels of our intellectuals to the mass of those taking even a slight interest in things and making some effort to think. This was precisely what happened with the European movement of the 1830s. Very quickly, right from the beginning of the thirties, we learned of this immense movement of European literatures. The names of the many newly fledged orators, historians, publicists, and professors became known. We even knew, though incompletely and superficially, the direction in which this movement was heading. And this movement manifested itself with particular passion in art – in the novel and above all in George Sand. It is true that Senkovsky and Bulgarin had warned the public about George Sand even before her novels appeared in Russian. They tried to frighten Russian ladies, in particular, by telling them that she wore trousers; they tried to frighten people by saying she was depraved; they wanted to ridicule her. Senkovsky, who himself had been planning to translate George Sand in his magazine *Reader's Library*, began calling her Mrs. Yegor Sand in print and, it seems, was truly pleased with his witticism. Later on, in 1848, Bulgarin wrote in *The Northern Bee* that she indulged in daily drinking bouts with Pierre Leroux somewhere near the city gates and participated in 'Athenian evenings' at the Ministry of the Interior; these evenings were supposedly hosted by the Minister himself, the bandit Ledru-Rollin. I read this myself and re-member it very clearly. But at that time, in 1848, nearly the whole of our reading public knew George Sand, and no one believed Bulgarin. She appeared in Russian translation for the first time around the middle of the thirties. It's a pity that I don't recall when her first work was translated into Russian and which it was; but the impression it made must have been all the more startling. I think that the chaste, sublime purity of her characters and ideals and the modest charm of the severe, restrained tone of her narrative must have struck everyone then as it did me, still a youth – and this was the woman who went about in trousers engaging in debauchery! I was sixteen, I think, when I read her tale *L'Uscoque* for the first time; it is one of the most charming among her early works. Afterward, I recall, I had a fever all night long. I think I am right in saying, by my recollection at least, that George Sand for some years held almost the first place in Russia among the whole Pleiad of new writers who had suddenly become famous and created such a stir all over Europe. Even Dickens, who appeared in Russia at virtually the same time, was perhaps not as popular among our readers as she. I am not including Balzac, who arrived before her but who produced works such as *Eugénie Grandet* and *Père Goriot* in the thirties (and to whom Belinsky was so unfair when he completely overlooked Balzac's significance in French literature). However, I say all this not to make any sort of critical evaluation but purely and simply to recall the tastes of the mass of Russian readers at that time and the direct impression these readers received. What mattered most was that the reader was able to derive, even from her novels, all the things the guardians were trying so hard to keep from them. At least in the

mid-forties the ordinary Russian reader knew, if only
incompletely, that George Sand was one of the bright-
est, most consistent, and most upright representatives
of the group of Western 'new people' of the time, who,
with their arrival on the scene, began to refute directly
those 'positive' achievements which marked the end of
the bloody French (or rather, European) revolution of
the preceding century. With the end of the revolution
(after Napoleon I) there were fresh attempts to express
new aspirations and new ideals. The most advanced
minds understood all too well that this had only been
despotism in a new form and that all that had happened was 'ôte toi de là que je m'y mette'; that the new
conquerors of the world, the bourgeoisie, turned out
to be perhaps even worse than the previous despots,
the nobility; that *Liberté, Égalité, Fraternité* proved
to be only a ringing slogan and nothing more. Moreover, certain doctrines appeared which transformed
such ringing slogans into utterly impossible ones. The
conquerors now pronounced or recalled these three
sacramental words in a tone of mockery; even science,
through its brilliant representatives (economists) came
with what seemed to be its new word to support this
mocking attitude and to condemn the utopian significance of these three words for which so much blood
had been shed. So it was that alongside the triumphant
conquerors there began to appear despondent and
mournful faces that frightened the victors. At this very
same time a truly new word was pronounced and hope

was reborn: people appeared who proclaimed directly that it had been vain and wrong to stop the advancement of the cause; that nothing had been achieved by the change of political conquerors; that the cause must be taken up again; that the renewal of humanity must be radical and social. Oh, of course, along with these solemn exclamations there came a host of views that were most pernicious and distorted, but the most important thing was that hope began to shine forth once more and faith again began to be regenerated. The history of this movement is well known; it continues even now and, it seems, has no intention of coming to a halt. I have no intention whatever of speaking either for or against it here, but I wanted only to define George Sand's real place within that movement. We must look for her place at the very beginning of the movement. People who met her in Europe then said that she was propounding a new status for women and foreseeing the 'rights of the free wife' (this is what Senkovsky said about her). But that was not quite correct, because she was by no means preaching only about women and never invented any notion of a 'free wife.' George Sand belonged to the whole movement and was not merely sermonizing on women's rights. It is true that as a woman she naturally preferred portraying *heroines* to *heroes*; and of course women all over the world should put on mourning in her memory, because one of the most elevated and beautiful of their representatives has died. She was, besides, a woman of almost unprecedented intelligence and talent – a name that has gone down in history, a name that is destined not to be forgotten and not to disappear from European humanity.

As far as her heroines are concerned, I repeat that from my very first reading at the age of sixteen I was amazed by the strangeness of the contradiction between what was written and said about her and what I myself could see in fact. In actual fact, many, or at least some, of her heroines represented a type of such sublime moral purity as could not be imagined without a most thorough moral scrutiny within the poet's own soul; without the acceptance of one's full responsibility; without an understanding and a recognition of the most sublime beauty and mercy, patience, and justice. It is true that along with mercy, patience, and the recognition of one's obligations there was also an extraordinary pride in this scrutiny and in protest, but this pride was precious because it stemmed from that higher truth without which humanity could never maintain its high moral ideals. This pride is not a feeling of hostility *quand même*, based on the fact that I am supposedly better than you and you are worse than I; it is only a sense of the most chaste impossibility of compromise with falsity and vice, although, I repeat, this feeling excludes neither universal forgiveness nor mercy. Moreover, along with the pride came an enormous responsibility, voluntarily assumed. These heroines of hers sought to make sacrifices and do noble

deeds. Several of the girls in her early works particularly appealed to me; these were the ones depicted, for
example, in what were called at the time her Venetian
tales (including *L'Uscoque* and *Aldini*). These were of
the type that culminated in her novel *Jeanne*, a brilliant work which presents a serene and, perhaps, a final
solution to the historical question of Joan of Arc. In
a contemporary peasant girl she suddenly resurrects
before us the image of the historical Joan of Arc and
graphically makes a case for the actual possibility of
this majestic and marvellous historical phenomenon, a
task quite characteristic of George Sand, for no one but
she among contemporary poets, perhaps, bore within
her soul such a pure ideal of an innocent girl, an ideal
that derives its power from its innocence. In several
works in succession we find all these girl characters
engaged in the same task and exemplifying the same
theme (however, not only girls: this same theme is repeated later in her magnificent novel *La Marquise*, also
one of her early works). We see depicted the upright,
honest, but inexperienced character of a young female
having that proud chastity, a girl who is unafraid and
who cannot be stained by contact with vice, even if she
were suddenly to find herself in some den of iniquity.
The need for some magnanimous sacrifice (which supposedly she alone must make) strikes the heart of the
young girl, and, without pausing to think or to spare
herself, she selflessly, self-sacrificingly, and fearlessly
takes a most perilous and fateful step. The things

she sees and encounters subsequently do not trouble or frighten her in the least; to the contrary, courage at once rises up in her young heart, which only now becomes fully aware of its power – the power of innocence, honesty, purity. Courage doubles her energy and shows new paths and new horizons to a mind that had not fully known itself but was vigorous and fresh and not yet stained by life's compromises. In addition to this, there was the irreproachable and charming form of her poem-novels. At that time George Sand was particularly fond of ending her poems *happily*, with the triumph of innocence, sincerity, and young, fearless simplicity. Are these images that could trouble society and arouse doubts and fears? To the contrary, the strictest fathers and mothers began permitting their families to read George Sand and could only wonder, 'Why is everyone saying these things about her?' But then voices of warning began to be heard: 'In this very pride of a woman's quest, in this irreconcilability of chastity with vice, in this refusal to make any concessions to vice, in this fearlessness with which innocence rises up to struggle and to look straight into the eyes of the offender – in all this there is a poison, the future poison of women's protest, of women's emancipation.' And what of it? Perhaps they were right about the poison; a poison really was being brewed, but what it sought to destroy, what had to perish from that poison and what was to be saved – these were the questions, and they were not answered for a long time.

Now these questions have long been resolved (or so it seems). It should be noted, by the way, that by the middle of the forties the fame of George Sand and the faith in the force of her genius stood so high that we, her contemporaries, all expected something incomparably greater from her in the future, some unprecedented new word, even something final and decisive. These hopes were not realized: it turned out that at that same time, that is, by the end of the forties, she had already said everything that she was destined to say, and now the final word about her can be said over her fresh grave.

George Sand was not a thinker, but she had the gift of most clearly intuiting (if I may be permitted such a fancy word) a happier future awaiting humanity. All her life she believed strongly and magnanimously in the realization of those ideals precisely because she had the capacity to raise up the ideal in her own soul. The preservation of this faith to the end is usually the lot of all elevated souls, all true lovers of humanity. George Sand died a *déiste*, firmly believing in God and her own immortal life, but it is not enough to say only that of her: beyond that she was, perhaps, the most Christian of all her contemporaries, the French writers, although she did not formally (as a Catholic) confess Christ. Of course, as a Frenchwoman George Sand, like her compatriots, was unable to confess consciously the idea that 'in all Creation there is no name other than His by which one may be saved' – the principal idea of Orthodoxy. Still, despite this apparent and formal contradiction, George Sand was, I repeat, perhaps one of the most thoroughgoing confessors of Christ even while unaware of being so. She based her socialism, her convictions, her hopes, and her ideals on the human moral sense, on humanity's spiritual thirst, on its striving toward perfection and purity, and not on the 'necessity' of the ant heap. She believed unconditionally in the human personality (even to the point of its immortality), and she elevated and expanded the conception of it throughout her life, in each of her works. Thus her thoughts and feelings coincided with one of the most basic ideas of Christianity, that is, the acknowledgment of the human personality and its freedom (and accordingly, its responsibility). From here arise her acknowledgment of duty and rigorous moral scrutiny to that end, along with a complete awareness of human responsibility. And there was not a thinker or writer in the France of her time, perhaps, who understood so clearly that 'man does not live by bread alone.' As far as the pride in her scrutiny and her protest are concerned, I repeat that this pride never excluded mercy, the forgiveness of an offence and even limitless patience based on compassion toward the one who gave offence. On the contrary, in her works George Sand was often attracted by the beauty of these truths and often created incarnations of the most sincere forgiveness and love. They write that she died as an admirable mother who worked to the end of her life, a friend to the local peasants, deeply beloved by her friends. It seems she was somewhat inclined to set great store by her aristocratic origins (she was descended on her mother's side from the royal house of Saxony), but, of course, one can state firmly that if she saw aristocracy as something to be valued in people, it was an aristocracy based only on the level of perfection of the human soul: she could not help but love the great, she could not reconcile herself with the base and compromise her ideas; and here, perhaps, she may have shown an excess of pride. It is true that she also did not like to portray humble people in her novels, to depict the just but pliant, the eccentric and the downtrodden, such as we meet in almost every novel of the great Christian Dickens. On the contrary, she proudly elevated her heroines and placed them as high as queens. This she loved to do, and this trait we should note; it is rather characteristic.

– My Paradox –
(June 1876)

Again a tussle with Europe (oh, it's not a war yet: they say that we – Russia, that is – are still a long way from war). Again the endless Eastern Question is in the news; and again in Europe they are looking mistrustfully at Russia . . . Yet why should we go running to seek Europe's trust? Did Europe ever trust the Russians? Can she ever trust us and stop seeing us as her enemy? Oh, of course this view will change *someday*; someday Europe will better be able to make us out and realize what we are like; and it is certainly worth discussing this *someday*; but meanwhile a somewhat irrelevant question or side issue has occurred to me and I have recently been busy trying to solve it. No one may agree with me, yet I think that I am right – in part, maybe, but right.

I said that Europe doesn't like Russians. No one, I think, will dispute the fact that they don't like us. They accuse us, among other things, of being terrible liberals: we Russians, almost to a man, are seen as not only liberals but revolutionaries; we are supposedly always inclined, almost lovingly, to join forces with the destructive elements of Europe rather than the conserving ones. Many Europeans look at us mockingly and haughtily for this – they are hateful: they cannot understand why we should be the ones to take the negative side *in someone else's affair*; they positively deny us the right of being negative as Europeans on the grounds that they do not recognize us as a part of 'civilisation'. They see us rather as barbarians, reeling around Europe gloating that we have found something somewhere to destroy – to destroy purely for the sake of destruction, for the mere pleasure of watching it fall to pieces, just as if we were a horde of savages, a band of Huns, ready to fall upon ancient Rome and destroy its sacred shrines without the least notion of the value of the things we are demolishing. That the majority of Russians have really proclaimed themselves liberals in Europe is true, and it is even a strange fact. Has anyone ever asked himself why this is so? Why was it that in the course of our century, virtually nine-tenths of the Russians who acquired their culture in Europe always associated themselves with the stratum of Europeans who were liberal, with the left – i.e., always with the side that rejected its own culture and its own civilisation? (I mean to a greater or a lesser degree, of course: what Thiers rejects in civilisation and what the Paris Commune of 1871 rejected are very different things). And like these European liberals, Russians in Europe are liberals 'to a greater or lesser degree' and in many different shades; but nonetheless, I repeat, they are more inclined than the Europeans to join directly with the extreme left at once rather than to begin by dwelling among the lesser ranks of liberalism. In short, you'll find far fewer Thierses than you will Communards among the Russians. And note that these are not some crowd of ragamuffins – not all of them, at least – but people with a very solid, civilised look about them, some of them almost like cabinet ministers. But Europeans do not trust appearances: 'Grattez le russe et vous verrez le tartare,' they say (scratch a Russian and you'll find a Tatar). That may be true, but this is what occurred to me: do the majority of Russians, in their dealings with Europe, join the extreme left because they are Tatars and have the savage's love of destruction, or are they, perhaps, moved by other reasons? That is the question, and you'll agree that it is a rather interesting one. The time of our tussles with Europe is coming to an end; the role of the window cut through to Europe is over, and something else is beginning, or ought to begin at least, and everyone who has the least capacity to think now realizes this. In short, we are more and more beginning to feel that we ought to be ready for something, for some new and far more original encounter with Europe than we have had hitherto. Whether that encounter will be over the Eastern Question or over something else no one can tell! And so it is that all such questions, analyses, and even surmises and paradoxes can be of interest simply through the fact that they can teach us something. And isn't it a curious thing that it is precisely those Russians who are most given to considering themselves Europeans, and whom we call 'Westernisers,' who exult and take pride in this appellation and who still taunt the other half of the Russians with the names 'kvasnik' and 'zipunnik?'[7] Is it not curious, I say, that these very people are the quickest to join the extreme left – those who deny civilisation and who would destroy it – and that this surprises absolutely no one in Russia, and that the question has never even been posed? Now isn't that truly a curious thing?

I'll tell you frankly that I have framed an answer to this question, but I don't intend to try to prove my idea. I shall merely explain it briefly in an effort to bring forth the facts. In any case, it cannot be proven, because there are some things which are incapable of proof.

This is what I think: does not this fact (i.e., the fact that even our most ardent Westernisers side with the extreme left – those who in essence reject Europe) reveal the protesting Russian soul which always, from the very time of Peter the Great, found many, all too many, aspects of European culture hateful and always alien? That is what I think. Oh, of course this protest was almost always an unconscious one; but what truly matters here is that the Russian instinct has not died: the Russian soul, albeit unconsciously, has protested precisely in the name of its Russianness, in the name of its downtrodden and Russian principle. People will

7 Derived from 'kvass,' a traditional Russian fermented drink, and 'zipun,' a peasant coat of rough homespun material.

say, of course, that if this really were so there would be
no cause for rejoicing: 'the one who rejects, be he Him,
barbarian, or Tatar, has rejected not in the name of
something higher but because he himself was so lowly
that even over two centuries he could not manage to
make out the lofty heights of Europe.'

People will certainly say that. I agree that this is a
legitimate question, but I do not intend to answer it;
I will only say, without providing any substantiation,
that I utterly and totally reject this Tatar hypothesis.
Oh, of course, who now among all us Russians, especially when this is all in the past (because this period
certainly has ended) – who, among all us Russians can
argue against the things that Peter did, against the
window he cut through to Europe? Who can rise up
against him with visions of the ancient Muscovy of the
tsars? This is not the point at all, and this is not why I
began my discussion; the point is that, no matter how
many fine and useful things we saw through Peter's
window, there still were so many bad and harmful
things there that always troubled the Russian instinct.
That instinct never ceased to protest (although it lost
its way so badly that in most cases it did not realize
what it was doing), and it protested not because of its
Tatar essence but, perhaps, precisely because it had
preserved something within itself that was higher and
better than anything it saw through the window (Well,
of course it didn't protest against everything: we received a great many fine things from Europe and we

don't want to be ungrateful; still, our instinct was right in protesting against at least half of the things.)

I repeat that all this happened in a most original fashion: it was precisely our most ardent Westernisers, precisely those who struggled for reform, who at the same time were rejecting Europe and joining the ranks of the extreme left . . . And the result: in so doing they defined themselves as the most fervent Russians of all, the champions of old Russia and the Russian spirit. And, of course, if anyone had tried to point that out to them at the time, they would either have burst out laughing or been struck with horror. There is no doubt that they were unaware of any higher purpose to their protest. On the contrary, all the while, for two whole centuries, they denied their own high-mindedness, and not merely their high-mindedness but their very self-respect (there were, after all, some such ardent souls!), and to a degree that amazed even Europe; yet it turns out that they were the very ones who proved to be genuine Russians. It is this theory of mine that I call my paradox.

Take Belinsky, for example. A passionate enthusiast by nature, he was almost the first Russian to take sides directly with the European socialists who had already rejected the whole order of European civilisation; meanwhile, at home, in Russian literature, he waged a war to the end against the Slavophiles, apparently for quite the opposite cause. How astonished he would have been had those same Slavophiles told him that he was the most ardent defender of the Russian truth, the distinctly Russian individual, the Russian principle, and the champion of all those things which he specifically rejected in Russia for the sake of Europe, things he considered only a fantasy. Moreover, what if they had proved to him that in a certain sense he was the one who was the real conservative, precisely because in Europe he was a socialist and a revolutionary? And in fact that is almost the way it was. There was one huge mistake made here by both sides, and it was made first and foremost in that all the Westernisers of that time confused Russia with Europe. They took Russia for Europe, and by rejecting Europe and her order they thought to apply that same rejection to Russia. But Russia was not Europe at all; she may have worn a European coat, but beneath that coat was a different creature altogether. It was the Slavophiles who tried to make people see that Russia was not Europe but a different creature altogether when they pointed out that the Westernisers were equating things that were dissimilar and incompatible and when they argued that something true for Europe was entirely inapplicable to Russia, in part because all the things the Westernisers wanted in Europe had already long existed in Russia, in embryo or potentiality at least. Such things even comprise Russia's essence, not in any revolutionary sense but in the sense in which the notions of universal human renewal should appear: in the sense of divine Truth, the Truth of Christ, which, God grant,

will someday be realized on earth and which is preserved in its entirety in Orthodoxy. The Slavophiles
urged people to study Russia first and then draw conclusions. But it was not possible to study Russia then
and, in truth, the means to do so were not available.
In any case, at that time who could know anything
about Russia? The Slavophiles, of course, knew a hundred times more than the Westernisers (and that was a
minimum), but even they almost had to feel their way,
engaging in abstract speculation and relying mainly
on their remarkable instincts. Learning something became possible only in the last twenty years: but who,
even now, knows anything about Russia? At most,
the basis for study has been set down, but as soon as
an important question arises we at once hear a clamour of discordant voices. Here we have the Eastern
Question coming up again: well, admit it, are there
many among us – and who are they? – who can agree
on this question and agree on its solution? And this in
such an important, momentous, and fateful national
question! But never mind the Eastern Question! Why
take up such big questions? Just look at the hundreds,
the thousands of our internal and everyday, current
questions: how uncertain everyone is; how poorly our
views are established; how little accustomed we are to
work! Here we see Russia's forests being destroyed;
both landowners and peasants are cutting down trees
in a kind of frenzy. One can state positively that timber
is being sold for a tenth of its value: can the supply

last for long? Before our children grow up there will be only a tenth of today's timber on the market. What will happen then? Ruination, perhaps. And meanwhile, try to say a word about curtailing the right to destroy our forests and what do you hear? On the one hand, that it is a state and a national necessity, and, on the other, that it is a violation of the rights of private property – two opposite notions. Two camps will at once form, and one still doesn't know where liberal opinion, which resolves everything, will side. Indeed, will there be only two camps? The matter will drag on for a long time. Someone made a witty remark in the current liberal spirit to the effect that there is no cloud without a silver lining, since cutting down all the Russian forests would at least have the positive value of eliminating corporal punishment: the district courts would have no switches to beat errant peasants. This is some consolation, of course, yet somehow it is hard to believe: even if the forests should disappear altogether, there would always be something to flog people with; they'd start importing it, I suppose. Now the Yids are becoming landowners, and people shout and write everywhere that they are destroying the soil of Russia. A Yid, they say, having spent capital to buy an estate, at once exhausts all the fertility of the land he has purchased in order to restore his capital with interest. But just try and say anything against this and the hue and cry will be at once raised: you are violating the principles of economic freedom and equal rights for all citizens. But what sort of equal rights are there here if it is a case of a clear and Talmudic *status in statu* above all and in the first place? What if it is a case not only of exhausting the soil but also of the future exhaustion of our peasant who, having been freed from the landowner will, with his whole commune, undoubtedly and very quickly now fall into a far worse form of slavery under far worse landowners – those same new landowners who have already sucked the juices from the peasants of western Russia, those same landowners who are now buying up not only estates and peasants but who have also begun to buy up liberal opinion and continue doing so with great success? Why do we have all these things? Why is there such indecisiveness and discord over each and every decision we make? (And please note that: it is true, is it not?) In my opinion, it is not because of our lack of talent and not because of our incapacity for work; it is because of our continuing ignorance of Russia, of its essence and its individuality, its meaning and its spirit, despite the fact that, compared with the time of Belinsky and the Slavophiles, we have had twenty years of schooling. Even more: in these twenty years of schooling the study of Russia has in fact been greatly advanced, while Russian instinct has, it seems, declined in comparison with the past. What is the reason for this? But if their Russian instinct saved the Slavophiles at that time, then that same instinct was present in Belinsky as well, and sufficiently present so that the Slavophiles might have considered him their best friend. I repeat, there was an enormous misunderstanding on both sides here. Not in vain did Apollon Grigorev, who also sometimes had rather acute insights, say that 'had Belinsky lived longer he would certainly have joined the Slavophiles'. He had a real idea there.

– The Boy Celebrating His Saint's Day –
(January 1877)

D o you remember Count Tolstoy's *Childhood and Youth*? It has a young boy in it, the hero of the whole poem. But he is not just a boy like the other children and like his brother Volodia. He's only about twelve, and his head and heart are already visited by thoughts and feelings unlike those of other children his age. He passionately abandons himself to his dreams and feelings, already aware that it is better to keep them to himself. His shy disposition to purity and his lofty pride prevent him from revealing them. He envies his brother and considers him incomparably higher than he, especially as regards adroitness and good looks; and yet he secretly senses that his brother is far beneath him in all respects; but he drives away this thought, which he considers mean. Too often he regards himself in the mirror and decides that he is repulsively ugly. Through his mind flashes the notion that no one loves him, that people despise him . . . In short, he is a rather unusual boy, and yet he belongs to that type of upper-middle landowning family that found its poet and historian, fully and completely – and in accordance with Pushkin's behest – in Count Leo Tolstoy. And so some guests arrive at their house

– a large, Moscow, family house; it is the saint's day of the boy's sister. Along with the adults arrive children – both boys and girls. Games and dancing begin. Our hero is awkward; he is the poorest dancer of all; he wants to show off his wit, but he fails – and in front of so many pretty girls; he has his perennial notion, his perennial suspicion that he is inferior to all of them. In despair he resolves to do something rash so as to impress them all. In front of all the girls and all those haughty older boys who take no account of him, he, like one possessed, with the feeling of one who hurls himself into a chasm that has suddenly opened before him, sticks his tongue out at his tutor and strikes him with all his might! 'Now everyone knows what sort of fellow he is! Now he's made a mark!' He is removed in disgrace and shut up in a storeroom. Feeling that he is ruined forever, the boy begins to dream: now he's run away from home; he's joined the army, and in battle he kills a host of Turks and falls from his wounds. 'Victory! Where is our saviour?' everyone cries, as they embrace and kiss him. And now he's in Moscow, walking along Tverskoi Boulevard with a bandaged arm; he meets the Emperor . . . And suddenly the thought that the door will open and his tutor will come in with a bundle of switches makes these dreams fly away like so much dust. New dreams begin. Suddenly he thinks up a reason why 'everyone so dislikes him': very likely he is a foundling, and they've never told him. His thoughts grow into a whirlwind: now he's dying; they come into the storeroom and find his body: 'The poor boy!' says everyone, pitying him. 'He was a good boy! You're the one who ruined his life,' says his father to the tutor and now the dreamer is choked with tears . . . This whole episode ends with the boy falling ill with fever and delirium. It is a remarkably important psychological study of the soul of a child, beautifully written.

I had a reason for bringing up this study in such detail. I had a letter from K——v that described the death of a child, also a twelve-year-old boy; and it is quite possible that there was something similar here. However, I shall quote portions of the letter without changing a single word. The *topic* is interesting.

On the 8th of November, after dinner, the news went round the city that there had been a suicide: a *twelve- or thirteen-year-old lad*, a student in a junior high school, had hanged himself. It happened this way. The teacher, whose lesson the victim had not studied that day, punished him by making him stay after school until five o'clock. The boy kept pacing the floor of the room; he happened to see the cord on a pulley; he untied it, fastened it to a nail on which the honour roll usually hung and which, for some reason, had not been put up that day, and he hanged himself. The janitor, who was washing floors in the other classrooms, spotted the unfortunate boy and ran to get the inspector. The inspector rushed in and pulled the boy from the noose, but they were unable to revive him . . . What is the reason for this suicide? The boy had never been rowdy and had shown no signs of vicious behavior; on the whole, he had been a good student, but in the period before the suicide he had received a few unsatisfactory marks from his teacher, for which he had been punished . . . People say that both the boy's father, who was very strict, and the boy were celebrating that day their common saint's day. Perhaps the young lad was dreaming with childish delight of how his mother, father, and little brothers and sisters would greet him at home . . . But here he is, having to sit all alone and hungry in an empty building thinking about his father's terrible wrath that he will have to face, and about the shame, humiliation and, perhaps, also the punishment he will have to bear. He knew of suicide as an alternative (and in our day what child does not?). One feels terrible pity for the deceased lad, and pity for the inspector, an excellent person and pedagogue who is adored by his pupils; one fears for the school that sees such things happen within its walls. What were the feelings of the classmates of the deceased when they learned of what had happened? And what of the other children who study there, some of whom are only tiny little things in the preparatory classes? Is such training not too stringent? Is there not too much significance given to grades – to 'Ds' and 'Fs' and to honour rolls from whose nails pupils hang themselves? Is there not too much formalism and arid lack of feeling when we deal with education?

Of course, one feels terribly sorry for the poor young lad who was celebrating his saint's day; but I shall not enter into a detailed commentary on the probable causes for this heartbreaking *incident*, and particularly not on the topic of 'grades', 'Ds,' 'excessive severity,' and so on. All those things existed formerly, without suicides, and so evidently the reason does not lie here. I chose the episode from Tolstoy's *Boyhood* because of the similarity between both cases, but there is also an enormous difference. There is no doubt that the young lad, Misha, who was celebrating his saint's day, killed himself not from anger and fear alone. Both these feelings – anger and morbid dread – are too simple and would most likely have been *a result in themselves*. However, the fear of punishment could also really have had an influence, especially given a state of morbid anxiety. But still, even with that, the feeling must have been much more complex, and again, it is very possible that what occurred was something akin to what Count Tolstoy described: that is, suppressed and still unconscious childish questions, a powerful sense of some oppressive injustice, an anguished, precocious and tormenting sense of one's own insignificance, a morbidly intensified question: 'Why do they *all* dislike me so?' There is the passionate longing to compel people to pity, which is the same as a passionate longing for love *from them all* – there are these things, and a great host of other complications and subtleties. The fact is that some or other of these subtleties certainly were involved; but there are also features of a new sort of reality quite different from that of the placid, middle-stratum Moscow landowning family whose way of life had long been solidly established and whose *historian* is our Count Leo Tolstoy, who, it seems, appeared just at the time when the former structure of the Russian nobility, established on the basis of old landowners' ways, had arrived at some new, still unknown but radical crisis, or at least at a point when it was to be totally recast into new, not yet manifest, almost entirely unknown forms. In the incident here, of the boy whose saint's day it was, one particular feature comes entirely from our time. Count Tolstoy's boy could dream, with bitter tears of enervated emotion in his heart, of how *they* would come in, find his dead body, and begin to love and pity him and blame themselves. He could even dream of killing himself, but only *dream*: the strict order of the historically configured noble family would have made its mark even in a twelve-year-old child and would not have allowed his *dream* to become *actuality*; the other child *dreamed it, and then he did it*. In pointing this out, however, I have in mind not only the current epidemic of suicides. One senses that something is not right here, that an enormous part of the Russian order of life has remained entirely without any observer and without any *historian*. At least it is clear that the life of the upper-middle level of our nobility, so vividly described by our writers, is already an insignificant and 'dissociated' corner of Russian life generally. Who, then, will be the *historian* of the other corners, of which, it seems, there are so awfully many? And if, within this chaos that has gone on for so long and that is particularly prevalent in the life of our society now – a life in which, perhaps, even an artist of Shakespearean proportions cannot find a normative law and a guiding thread – who, then, will illuminate even a little part of this chaos, never mind dreaming of some guiding thread? The main thing is that it seems no one is capable of doing this; it is as if it were still too early even for our greatest artists. One cannot deny that a way of life in Russia is disintegrating; consequently, family life disintegrates as well. But certainly there is also a life that is being formed anew, on new principles. Who will pick these out and show them to us? Who can, even in small measure, define and express the laws of this disintegration and this new formation? Or is it still too early? But have we even taken complete note of what is old and past?

EDITOR'S NOTE

I. Despite the categorical statement in my December *Diary*, people continue to send me letters asking whether I will be publishing the new magazine, *Light*; they even enclose postage stamps for my reply. To all who have been enquiring I announce once more, and for the last time, that it is not I who will publish the magazine *Light* but Nikolai Petrovich Wagner, and that I will play no part in editing it.

II. Miss O. A. An——ova, who wrote to the editor regarding study for her examinations, is requested to supply her correct address. The address on Mokhovaia Street that she provided earlier proved to be incorrect.

– The Dream of a Ridiculous Man –
A FANTASTIC STORY
(April 1877)

I

I am a ridiculous man. They call me a madman now. It would have been a promotion for me had I not appeared as ridiculous to them as ever. But I no longer mind – they are all dear to me now, even when they are laughing at me, something endears them to me particularly then. I would laugh with them – not at myself, that is, but because I love them – I would laugh if I did not feel so sad looking at them. What saddens me is that they do not know the truth, and I do. Oh, how hard it is to be the only one to know the truth! But they will not understand this. No, they will not.

It used to hurt me very much that I seemed ridiculous. I did not seem it, I was. I have always been ridiculous and I think I've known it since the day I was born. I believe I realised it when I was seven, I went to school and then to the university, but what of it? The more I studied the more I came to realise that I was ridiculous. And so, as far as I was concerned, the ultimate meaning of science was to prove and explain to me, the more I probed it, that I was indeed ridiculous. Life taught me the same thing. With every year my awareness of how ridiculous I was in every respect grew and developed. I was laughed at by everyone and all the time. But none of them knew or guessed that of all the people in the world I knew best how ridiculous I was, and it was the fact that they did not know this that hurt me most of all, but the fault was entirely mine: I was always so proud that I would never admit this knowledge to anyone. My pride swelled in me with the years, and had I allowed myself to admit to anyone that I was ridiculous, I believe I would have blown my brains out that same night. Oh, the torment I went through in my adolescence for fear that I would weaken and make the admission to my friends! As I grew to manhood I learned more and more of this awful shortcoming of mine with every year, but in spite of this I took it a little more calmly for some reason. I repeat – for some reason, because to this day I fail to give it a clear definition. Perhaps it was because of that hopeless sadness that was mounting in my soul about something that was infinitely greater than myself: this something was a mounting conviction that *nothing mattered*. I had begun to suspect this long ago, but positive conviction came to me all at once, one day last year. I suddenly knew that I would *not have cared* if the world existed at all or if there was nothing anywhere. I began to know and feel with all my being that there has been *nothing since I have been there*. At first I kept thinking that there must have been a great deal before, but then I realised that there had not been anything before either, and that it only seemed so for some reason. Gradually, I became convinced that there would never be anything at all. It was then I suddenly ceased minding people and no longer noticed them at all. It was quite true, even in the merest trifles: for instance, I would walk into people as I went along the street. Not that I was lost in thought either, for what was there to think about, I had given up thinking altogether then: *I did not care.* Neither did I solve any problems; no, not a single one, and yet there was a host of them. But I did not care now, and all the problems receded into the background.

And it was much later that I learned the Truth. It was in November, the third of November to be exact, that I learned the Truth, and since then I remember every moment of my life. It happened on a gloomy night, the gloomiest night that could ever be. I was walking home, the time being after ten, and I remember thinking that no hour could be gloomier. It was so even physically. It had been raining all day, and it was the coldest and gloomiest rain, even an ominous rain, I remember, obviously hostile to people, and suddenly after ten it stopped and a horrible dampness set in, which was colder and damper than during the rain, and steam rose from everything, from every cobblestone, from every alleyway if you peered into his deepest and darkest recesses. I suddenly fancied that if all the gas-lights were to go out it would be more cheerful, for gas-light, showing up all this, made one feel even sadder. I had hardly eaten anything that day, and since late afternoon I had been at an engineer's I knew, with two other friends of his. I said nothing all evening and I believe I bored them. They were discussing something exciting and actually lost their tempers over it. They did not care, I could see, but lost their tempers just like that. I went and blurted it out to them: 'Gentlemen,' I said, 'you don't really care, you know.' They took no offence, they just laughed at me. That was because there was no sting in my remark, I simply made it because I did not care. They saw that I did not care and it made them laugh.

When, walking home, I thought of the gas-light, I glanced up at the sky. The sky was terribly dark, but I could clearly make out the ragged clouds and the fathomless black pits between them. Suddenly I noticed a tiny star twinkling in one of those pits and I stopped to stare at it. That was because the tiny star gave me an idea: I made up my mind to kill myself that night. I had made up my mind to do it fully two months before, and poor though I am I had bought a splendid revolver and had loaded it that same day. Two months had already passed, however, and it was still lying in my desk drawer; my feeling of not caring had been so strong then that I wanted to choose a moment when it would be a little less so to do it in, why – I do not know. And so every night, for two months, I had gone home with the thought of killing myself. I was watching for the right moment. And now this star gave me the idea, and I made up my mind that it *had to be* that night. I do not know why the tiny star gave me the idea.

There I stood staring at the sky when suddenly the little girl clutched at my arm. The street was already deserted and there was hardly a soul about. A droshky was standing some way off with the driver dozing in it. The girl must have been about eight. All she wore in this cold was a poor cotton frock and a kerchief, she was drenched through, but I particularly noticed her sodden, broken shoes. I remember them even now. They struck me particularly. She suddenly began to tug at my elbow and cry. She was not weeping, but was crying out snatches of words which she could not articulate properly because she was shivering all over as in a fever. Something had frightened her, and she called out desperately: 'My mummy, my mummy!' I half-turned towards her but said not a word and continued on my way, while she kept running after me, tugging at my coat, and her voice rang with that peculiar sound which in badly frightened children means despair. I know that sound. Though her words were incoherent, I understood that her mother lay dying somewhere, or perhaps it was some other disaster that had befallen them, and she had rushed out into the street to find someone or something to help her mother. But I did not go with her; on the contrary, it suddenly occurred to me to drive her away. I told her to go and look for a policeman. But she folded her hands in entreaty and, sobbing and panting, ran along at my side and would not leave me alone. It was then I stamped my feet at her and shouted. All she cried was: 'Sir, oh sir!' but, abandoning me abruptly, she darted across the street: another passer-by appeared there and it was to him she must have run from me.

I climbed my five flights of stairs. I live in a lodging house. My room is wretched and small, with just one attic window in it, a semicircular one. The furniture consists of an oilcloth-covered sofa, two chairs, a table with my books on it, and an armchair, a very, very old one but a Voltaire armchair for all that. I sat down, lighted my candle, and gave myself up to thought. The room next door was a real Bedlam. It has been going on since the day before yesterday. The man who lives there is a discharged captain and he was having guests, about six of them – castaways on the sea of life – drinking vodka and playing stoss with an old deck of cards. There had been a fight the night before, and I know that two of them had torn at one another's hair for quite a long time. The landlady wanted to put in a complaint against them, but she is terribly afraid of the captain. The only other lodger is a thin little lady, an officer's wife, a newcomer to the town with three small children, who have all been ill since they came here. The lady and the children live in deadly fear of the captain, they spend their nights shaking with fear and praying, and as for the youngest baby, it was even frightened into a fit once. The captain, I know for a fact, sometimes accosts people on the Nevsky and begs alms. He won't be given a post anywhere, but strangely (this is why I am telling all this), in all the months he has been staying with us, he never once roused any resentment in me. I naturally shunned his company from the outset, but then he too thought me a bore the very first time we met, and no matter how loudly they shout in their room or how many they are – I never care. I sit up all night and, honestly, I never even hear them, so utterly do I forget them. I cannot sleep, you know; it has been like that for a year now. I spend the night sitting in my armchair and doing nothing. I only read in the daytime. I just sit there, without even thinking. My thoughts are vague and stray, and I let them wander. My candle burns down every night. And so, I calmly settled down in my chair, took out my revolver and placed it on the table before me. I remember asking myself as I put it down: 'Are you sure?' and answering very firmly: 'I am sure.' That is, I would kill myself. I knew that I would definitely kill myself that night, but how much longer I would sit thus at the table before I did it I did not know. And I would have certainly killed myself if it had not been for that little girl.

II

You see how it was: though I did not care, I was still sensitive to pain, for instance. If someone struck me I would feel the pain. Mentally it was exactly the same: if something very pathetic happened I would feel pity, just as I would have felt pity in the days before I had ceased caring for anything in the world. And I did feel pity earlier that night: surely, I should have helped a child in distress? Why had I not helped her then? Because of a thought that had occurred to me; when she was tugging at my coat and crying out, a problem suddenly confronted me and I was unable to solve it. It was an idle problem but it had angered me. I got angry because, having definitely decided to commit suicide that very night, I ought to have cared less than ever for anything in the world. Then why had I suddenly felt that I did care and was sorry for the little girl? I remember I was frightfully sorry for her, my pity was strangely poignant and incongruous in my position. I really cannot give a better description of that fleeting feeling of mine, but it remained with me even after I had reached my room and had seated myself in my chair, and it vexed me more than anything else had done for a long time. One argument followed another. It was perfectly clear to me that if I was a man and not yet a nought, and had not yet become a nought, I was therefore alive and, consequently, able to suffer, resent, and feel shame for my actions. Very well. But if I was going to kill myself in a couple of hours from then, why should I be concerned with the girl and what did I care for shame or anything else in the world? I would become a nought, an absolute nought. And could it be that my ability to feel pity for the girl and shame for my vile action was not in the least affected by the certainty that I would soon become completely non-existent, and therefore nothing would exist. Why, the reason I had stamped my feet and shouted so brutally at the poor child was to assert that: 'Far from feeling pity, I could even afford to do something inhumanly vile now, because two hours hence all would fade away.' Do you believe me when I say that this was the reason why I had shouted? I am almost positive now that it was that. It had seemed clear to me that life and the world were from then on dependent on me, as it were. I should even say that the world seemed specially made for me alone: if I killed myself the world would be no more, at least as far as I was concerned. To say nothing of the possibility that there would really be nothing for anyone after I was gone, and the moment my consciousness dimmed the whole world, being a mere attribute of my consciousness, would instantly dim too, fade like a mirage and be no more, for it may be that all this world of ours and all these people are merely part of myself, are just myself. I remember that as I sat there and reasoned, I gave an entirely different twist to all these new problems that were thronging my mind, and conceived some perfectly new ideas. For instance, a strange notion like this occurred to me: supposing I had once lived on the moon or Mars and had there committed the foulest and scurviest of deeds imaginable, for which I had been made to suffer all the scorn and dishonour conceivable in nothing less than in a dream, in a night-mare, and supposing I later found myself on the earth, with the crime committed on that other planet alive in my consciousness and, besides, knowing there was no return for me, ever, under any circumstances – would I have *cared* or not as I gazed at the moon from this earth? Would I have felt shame for that deed or not? All these questions were idle and superfluous since the revolver was already lying in front of me and I knew with all my being *that it was bound to happen*, and yet the questions excited me and roused me to a frenzy. I no longer seemed able to die before I had solved something first. In short, that little girl saved my life because the unsolved questions put off the act. Meanwhile, the noise at the captain's began to subside too: they had finished their game and were now settling down to sleep, grumbling, and sleepily rounding off their mutual abuse. It was then that I suddenly fell asleep in my chair in front of the table, a thing that never happened to me before. I dropped off without knowing it at all. Dreams, we all know, are extremely queer things: one will be appallingly vivid, with the greatest imaginable precision in every minutely finished detail, while another will take you through time and space so swiftly that you hardly notice the flight. Dreams, I believe, are directed by desire, not reason, by the heart and not the mind, and yet what fantastic tricks my reason sometimes plays on me in dreams! The things that happen to my reason in sleep are quite incredible. To give an instance: my brother has been dead these five years. I dream of him sometimes: he takes an active interest in my affairs, we are very fond of one another, yet all through my dream I know perfectly well that my brother has long been dead and buried. Why does it not surprise me then that though dead he is still there beside me, worrying about my affairs? Why does my reason reconcile itself to all this so willingly? But enough. To return to my dream. Yes, my dream of November the 3rd. They all tease me now that, after all, it was nothing but a dream. But surely it makes no difference whether it was a dream or not since it did reveal the Truth to me? Because if you have come to know it once and to see it, you will know it is the Truth and that there is not, there cannot be any other, whether you are dreaming or living. Very well, it was a dream – let it be a dream, but the fact remains that I was going to snuff out the life which you all extol so, whereas my dream, my dream – oh, my dream revealed to me another life, a life revived, magnificent and potent.

Listen then.

III

I said that I fell asleep without knowing it and even continuing with my musings on the same matters when no longer awake, as it were. A dream came to me that I picked up my revolver and, still keeping my chair, pressed it to my heart – my heart and not my head, whereas I had definitely decided to shoot myself through the head, and the right temple it had to be. With the revolver pressed to my heart I waited a moment or two, and suddenly my candle, the table and the wall in front of me all began to rock and sway. I quickly pulled the trigger.

In dreams you sometimes fall from a great height or you are stabbed or beaten, but you never feel the pain unless you jerk and actually hurt yourself against the bedpost; you do feel the pain then, and it is almost certain to wake you up. It was the same in my dream: I felt no pain but with the sound of the report my whole being seemed to be shaken up and suddenly everything was extinguished and there was a horrible blackness all around me. I seemed to have gone blind and mute, I was lying on something very hard, stretched out on my back, seeing nothing and unable to make the slightest movement. Voices shouted and feet tramped all about me; there was the captain's low rumble and the landlady's shrill screech – and suddenly there was a blank again, and now they were carrying me in a coffin with the lid nailed down. I could feel the coffin swaying and I was reflecting upon it, when all of a sudden the thought struck me for the first time: I was dead, quite dead. I knew it without a doubt, I could neither see nor move, and yet I could feel and reason. But soon I reconciled myself to this and, as usual in dreams, accepted the fact without demur.

And now they were piling earth over my grave. Everyone left, I was alone, utterly alone. I did not stir. Whenever I used to imagine what it would be like to be buried, I generally associated but one sensation with the grave: the feeling of damp and cold. And now too I felt very cold, the tips of my toes were the worst, and that was all the sensation I had.

I lay there and, strangely, expected nothing, resigning myself to the fact that the dead have nothing to expect. But it was damp. I do not know how long I lay there – whether it was an hour, or a day, or many days. All of a sudden a drop of water, which had seeped through the lid of the coffin, fell on my left closed eye; a minute later there was another drop, a minute more and there was a third, and so on, drops falling at regular one-minute intervals. Indignation mounted in my heart, and suddenly I felt a physical pain in it. 'It's my wound,' I thought. 'My shot, the bullet's there . . .' And the water kept dripping, a drop a minute, straight down on my closed eye. I suddenly invoked, not with my voice for I lay inert, but with the whole of my being, the Ruler of all that was befalling me: 'Whoever Thou may be, but if Thou art and if there does exist any wisdom greater than the present, suffer it to descend upon this too. But if Thou art imposing vengeance upon me for my unwise suicide, with all the ugliness and incongruity of the life to come, then know Thee that no tortures I could ever be made to suffer could compare with the contempt I shall always feel in silence, be it through millions of years of martyrdom!'

I invoked and fell silent. Deep silence reigned for almost a full minute, and one more drop fell, but I knew with infinite and profound faith, that all would be different now. And suddenly my grave was rent open. That is, I do not know if it was dug open, but a dark and strange being picked me up and bore me away into space. I suddenly recovered sight. It was deep night, and never, never had there been such darkness yet! We were flying through space, the earth was already far behind us. I asked the one that bore me nothing at all, I waited, I was proud. I made myself believe I was not afraid, and my breath caught with admiration at the thought that I was not afraid. I do not remember how long we flew nor can I venture a guess: everything was happening the way it usually happens in dreams when you leap over space and time, over all laws of life and reason, and only pause where your heart's desire bids you pause. I remember I suddenly saw a tiny star in the darkness. 'Is it Sirius?' I could not hold back the question, although I did not want to ask anything at all. 'No, that is the star you saw between the clouds on your way home,' replied the one that bore me away. I knew the being was somewhat human in likeness. Strangely enough, I had no love for that being, I rather felt a deep aversion for it. I had expected complete non-existence and with that thought I had shot myself. And now I was in the hands of a being, not a human being of course, but a *being* nonetheless that was, that existed. 'It just shows that there is life hereafter,' I thought with the peculiar flippancy of dreams, but the essence of my spirit remained with me intact. 'If I must *be* again,' I thought, 'and again live by someone's inescapable will, I do not want to be beaten and humiliated!' 'You know that I am afraid of you, and for this you despise me,' I suddenly said, unable to hold back my cringing words which held an admission, and feeling the pin-prick of humiliation in my heart. There was no reply, but all at once I knew that I was not being despised; I was not being laughed at nor even pitied; I knew that our flight through space had a purpose, mysterious and strange, concerning me alone. Fear mounted in my heart. Something was being mutely but painfully transmitted to me by my silent companion, piercing me through as it were. We flew through dark and unfamiliar space. I no longer saw the constellations my eyes were used to seeing. I knew that there were certain stars in the vastness of the sky whose rays took thousands and millions of years to reach the earth. Perhaps we were already flying through those regions. I waited for I knew not what, my tormented heart gripped with a terrible anguish. And suddenly I was shaken with a feeling that was familiar and so stirring: I saw our sun! I knew it could not be our sun which had begotten our earth, and also that we were infinitely far away from our sun, but my whole being told me that this was a sun exactly like our own, a duplicate of it, its twin. My soul rang with sweet and stirring ecstasy: this familiar source of light, the same light that had given me life, evoked an echo in my heart and resurrected it, and for the first time since my burial I sensed life, the same life as before.

'But if this is the sun, if this is a sun exactly like ours, then where is the earth?' I cried. And my companion pointed to a star sparkling in the darkness like emerald. We were flying straight towards it.

'Are such duplications really possible in the universe, is this really the law of nature? And if that star is an earth, can it be an earth like ours . . . exactly like ours, wretched and poor but dear and ever beloved, inspiring even in its most ungrateful children a love as poignant for it as our own earth inspires?' I cried out, trembling with rapturous, boundless love for that dear, old earth I had deserted. A vision of the poor little girl I had hurt flashed past me.

'You shall see everything,' my companion said, and I sensed a peculiar sorrow in his words. But now we were quickly nearing the planet. It grew as we approached, I could already distinguish the oceans, the outline of Europe, and suddenly my heart was ablaze with a great and holy jealousy. 'How can such a duplication be and what for? I do love and can love only the earth I have left behind, the earth bespattered with my blood when I in my ingratitude snuffed out my life with a shot through the heart. But I never, never ceased to love that earth, and the night I parted with it I think I loved it even more poignantly than ever before. Does this new earth hold suffering? On our earth we can only love truly by suffering and only through suffering. We can love in no other way and know no other love. I must have suffering, if I would love. I want, I long this instant to kiss that one and only earth I left behind me, and weep, and I do not want, I defy, life on any other!'

But my companion had already left me. I do not know how it came about but suddenly I found myself upon this other earth in the bright sunlight of a day as lovely as paradise. I believe I was on one of those islands which on our earth comprise the Greek Archipelago, or it may have been on the mainland somewhere, on the shore which the Archipelago adjoins. Everything was exactly the same as on our earth, but it all seemed to wear the splendour of a holiday, and shone with the glory of a great and holy triumph at last attained. A gentle emerald-green sea softly lapped the shores and caressed them with a love that was undisguised, visible, and almost conscious. Tall and beautiful trees stood in flowering splendour, while their countless little leaves welcomed me (I'm certain of it) with their gentle and soothing rustling, and they seemed to be murmuring words of love to me. The meadow was ablaze with bright, fragrant flowers. Birds fluttered above in flocks and unafraid of me alighted on my shoulders and hands and happily beat me with their sweet, tremulous wings. And finally I saw and came to know the people of this joyous land. They came to me themselves, they surrounded me and kissed me. Children of the sun, of their own sun – oh how beautiful they were! I have never seen such beauty in man on our planet. Only in our youngest children could one, perhaps, detect a distant and very faint reflection of this beauty. The eyes of these happy people shone with a clear light. Their faces were aglow with wisdom and intelligence matured into serenity, but their expression was gay; their words and voices rang with child-like joy. Oh, I instantly understood all, all, the moment I looked into their faces! This was an earth undefiled by sin, inhabited by people who had not sinned; they dwelt in a Garden of Eden just like the one in which our ancestors, so the legends of all mankind say, had once dwelt before they knew sin, with the only difference that the whole of this earth was one great Garden of Eden. These people, laughing happily, clung to me and caressed me; they led me away and every one of them showed eagerness to comfort me. They did not question me about anything at all, they seemed to know all, and were anxious to drive the suffering from my face.

IV

I repeat, you see: let it be nothing but a dream. But the sensation of being loved by those innocent and beautiful people will remain with me for ever, and even now I can feel their love pouring down on me from up there. I have seen them with my own eyes, have known them and been convinced; I have loved them and, afterwards, suffered for them. Oh, I realised from the first that I should never be able to understand them at all in many things; for instance, it appeared inexplicable to me, a modern Russian progressive and wretched citizen of St Petersburg, that, knowing so much, they did not possess our science. But I soon realised that their knowledge was enriched and stimulated by other penetrations than ours, and that their aspirations were also quite different from ours. They desired nothing and were content, they did not strive to know life the way we strive to probe its depths, because their life was consummate. Their knowledge was finer and more profound than our science, for our science attempts to explain the meaning of life. Science itself strives to fathom it in order to teach others how to live; while they knew how to live without the help of science, I saw it but I could not understand this knowledge of theirs. They showed their trees to me, and I failed to appreciate the depth of the love with which they gazed at them: it was as if they were speaking to beings like themselves. And do you know, I may not be wrong if I tell you that they did speak to them. Yes, they had found a common tongue and I am convinced the trees understood them. This was the way they treated all Nature – the beasts who lived in peace with them, never attacking them and loving them, conquered by the people's own love for them. They pointed out the stars to me and spoke to me about them, saying things I could not understand, but I am positive they had some tie with those heavenly bodies, a living tie, not spiritual alone. Oh no, these people did not insist that I should understand them, they loved me as it was, but then I knew that they, too, would never understand me and so hardly spoke to them about our earth. I only kissed the earth they lived on and without words adored them, and they saw it and permitted themselves to be adored, unashamed of my adoration, for their own love was great. They felt no pang for me when, moved to tears, I sometimes kissed their feet, joyfully certain in my heart of the infinite love with which they would reciprocate my emotion. I sometimes asked myself in bewilderment: how was it that they never insulted one like me, never roused one like me to feelings of jealousy or envy? I asked myself again and again, how did I, a braggart and a liar, refrain from telling them of all my acquired knowledge of which they naturally had no inkling, from wishing to impress them with it, if only because I loved them? They were gay and frolicsome like children. They wandered about their beautiful groves and forests, singing their beautiful songs, eating light food – the fruit of their trees, the honey of their woods, and the milk of the beasts devoted to them. They toiled but little to procure their food and clothing. They loved and begot children, but never did I detect any signs of that cruel sensuality in them, which almost everyone falls victim to on our earth, one and all, and which serves as the sole source of almost all the sins of mankind on our earth. They welcomed the children born to them as new participants in their bliss. There were no quarrels or jealousy among them, and they did not even understand the meaning of these words. Their children were the children of all of them, for they formed one family. Sickness was very rare, though there was death; but their old people died peacefully; they seemed to fall asleep, blessing and smiling upon the ones they were taking leave of, themselves carrying away the clear smiles of those surrounding them in farewell. I saw no grief or tears then, only love multiplied as it were to ecstasy, but an ecstasy that was serene, contemplative and consummate. It was as if they kept in touch with their dead even after their death, and that their earthly ties were un-severed by death. They hardly understood me when I asked them if they believed in life eternal, for evidently their faith in it was so implicit it presented no problem to them. They had no churches, but they had a vital, close and constant association with the Sum of the universe; they had no creed, but instead they had the unshakable knowledge that, when their earthly bliss was consummated to the ultimate extent of its earthly nature, all of them – the living and the dead – would come into even closer contact with the Sum of the universe. They looked forward to that day with eagerness but with no impatience or morbid longing. It seemed rather that they were already carrying a foretaste of it in their hearts, sharing it with one another. Before going to sleep at night they would sing, their voices blending in true and blissful harmony. Their songs spoke of all that the passing day had granted them to feel, they hallowed it and bid it farewell. They hallowed nature, earth, sea and woods. They were fond of making up songs about one another, praising one another like children; they were the simplest of songs, but they came from the heart and stirred other hearts. Why songs alone? Their very lives were spent admiring one another. It was a sort of infatuation with one another, universal and complete. However, some of their other songs, solemn and exultant, I hardly understood at all. While understanding the words, I could never grasp their full meaning. It remained beyond my intelligence, as it were, yet instinctively my heart grew more and more responsive to it. I often told them that I had fore-glimpsed this long, long ago; that all this happiness and glory had stirred a chord of anguished longing in me while on our own planet, mounting at times to unbearable sorrow; that I had fore-glimpsed all of them and their glory in the dreams of my heart and the visions of my mind; that often I could not watch the sun go down on our earth without tears . . . That my hatred for the people on our earth always held sadness: why could I not hate them without loving them, why could I not help forgiving them, and why was there sadness in my love for them; why could I not love them without hating them? They listened to me, and I saw that they could not comprehend what I was telling them, but I was not sorry I had told them for I knew that they appreciated to the full the great yearning I felt for the ones I had left behind. When they turned their dear, loving gaze on me, when I felt that with them my heart became as innocent and truthful as theirs, it sufficed me, and I was not sorry I did not understand them. I was speechless with the fullness of life, and could only worship them in silence.

Oh, everyone laughs in my face now and says that one could never dream of all those details I am narrating now, that in my dream I could have seen and felt nothing but a mere sensation of something conceived by my own heart in delirium, and as for the details I must have made them up on awakening. And when I admitted to them that it may really have been so – oh Lord, the way they laughed in my face, the fun they had at my expense! Yes, of course, I was overcome by the mere Sensation of my dream, and that alone survived in my wounded, bleeding heart: as for the actual images and shapes, that is, those I had really seen in my dream, they were so perfect in their harmony, charm and beauty and were so true, that our feeble words naturally failed me to describe them on awakening, and they were bound to become blurred in my mind. Therefore, I may indeed have been compelled to make up the details afterwards though unconsciously, distorting them of course, especially since I was so impatient and eager to give them some sort of expression. But then how could I doubt the truth of my words? It was a thousand times better perhaps, brighter and happier than I am telling it. Granted it was a dream, but all of this had been, it had to be. Do you know, I shall tell you a secret: it may not have been a dream at all! Because something happened next, something so horribly true that it could never come to one even in a dream. Granted, my heart conceived that dream, but could my heart alone have been able to conceive that appalling reality which befell me next? How could I have made it up by myself, how could my heart prompt that dream? Surely my shallow heart and my whimsical, wretched mind could not have been elevated to such revelations of the truth? Oh, judge for yourselves: I have concealed it until now, but now I shall disclose this truth as well. The fact is that I . . . I corrupted them all!

V

Yes, yes, it ended in my corrupting them all! I do not know how it could have happened, but I remember perfectly that it did. My dream sped across thousands of years and left with me only an impression of it as a whole. I only know that it was I who caused their downfall. Like a malignant trichina, an atom of the plague afflicting whole kingdoms, so I spread contamination through all that happy earth, sinless before I came to it. They learned to lie and came to love lying, appreciating the beauty of lies. Oh, it may have begun quite *innocently*, with laughter, coquetry, playful love, or it really may have been the atom of lying seeping into their hearts and appealing to them. Soon after, sensuality was born, sensuality conceived jealousy, and jealousy conceived cruelty . . . Oh, I don't know, I can't remember, but soon, very soon blood was spilt for the first time: they were astounded and horrified, and began to separate and go different ways. They formed unions, but the unions were inimical to one another. Reproaches and recriminations began. They came to know shame and made a virtue of it. They learned the meaning of honour, and each union flew its own colours. They became cruel to their beasts who retreated from them into the forests and turned hostile. A struggle ensued for division, for sovereignty, for personal prominence, for thine and mine. They now spoke different tongues. They tasted of sorrow and came to love sorrow, they thirsted for sufferings and said that only through suffering could Truth be attained. And then science was introduced. When they grew evil, they began to talk of fraternity and humanity and understood these precepts. When they grew criminal they invented the idea of justice and in order to maintain it prescribed for themselves voluminous codes of law, and to add security to these codes they erected a guillotine. They had but a vague memory of what they had lost, and even refused to believe that once they had been innocent and happy. The very thought that they could have once been so happy made them laugh, and they called it a dream. They could not even envisage it in images and shapes, but strangely and miraculously, though they had lost all faith in their former happiness

calling it a fairy-tale, they so wanted to become innocent and happy again that they succumbed to their
heartfelt wish like children and, deifying this wish,
they put up numerous temples and began to pray to
their own idea, or rather their 'wish,' knowing full well
that it could never come true or be granted to them,
but adoring and worshipping it in tears none the less.
And yet, if it had been possible to restore them to the
innocent and happy realm they had lost, or if someone could have given them a glimpse of it again and
asked them whether they would like to come back to
it, they would have probably refused. They told me:
'Let us be deceitful, evil and unjust, but we know it,
we weep over it, and torment ourselves for it, and the
punishment we inflict upon ourselves is even harsher
perhaps than that which will be meted out to us by
the merciful Judge who will sit in judgement over us
and whose name we do not know. We possess science,
and through it we shall seek and find the Truth once
again, and this time we shall apprehend it consciously.
Knowledge is superior to feeling, consciousness of life
is superior to life. Science will give us wisdom, wisdom
will determine the laws, and knowledge of the laws of
happiness is superior to happiness.' This is what they
said to me, and after saying it each one loved himself
above all others, nor could he have done differently.
Each one protected his ego so jealously, that he directed all his strivings towards humiliating and belittling
the ego of others: and this became his life work. Next

came slavery, there was voluntary slavery as well: the weak willingly submitted to the strong only so they should help them to crush those even weaker than themselves. There were the righteous who came to these people and in tears spoke to them of their arrogance, of their loss of all sense of measure and harmony, all shame. But the righteous were mocked and stoned. Holy blood dyed the thresholds of temples. Men appeared in their stead who began to contrive how best to unite everyone once again but in such a manner that each should continue loving himself above all others and yet should not stand in the others' way, so that all could once more live together in apparently good agreement. Great wars were fought because of this idea. Though engaged in warfare, the fighters firmly believed that science, wisdom and the instinct of self-preservation would eventually force mankind to unite into a society that was concordant and sensible, and in the meantime, to speed matters up, the 'wise' tried to exterminate the unbelievers in their idea and the 'unwise' as quickly as possible so they should not impede the idea's triumph. But the instinct of self-preservation soon began to weaken, and men pandering to their arrogance or sensuality demanded outright: all or nothing. To acquire all they resorted to crime and if that failed – to suicide. Religions were next introduced with a cult of non-existence and self-destruction for the sake of eternal peace in nonentity. The people were at last worn out with their senseless toil, and suffering shadowed their faces; and they proclaimed that suffering was beauty, for in suffering alone lay thought. They extolled suffering in their songs. I walked among them, wringing my hands and weeping over them; my love for them was even greater perhaps than before when their faces showed no suffering and they were innocent and so beautiful. I came to love the earth defiled by them even more than I did when it was a paradise, solely because grief had come to it. Alas, I have always loved sorrow and grief, but for my own self, for myself alone, while over them I wept in pity. I held my arms out to them in despair, accusing, cursing and despising myself. I told them that I had done it all, I alone; that it was I who brought them this germ of corruption, iniquity and deceit. I implored them to crucify me, I taught them how to make the cross. I could not, I had not the strength to kill myself, but I wanted to suffer at their hands, I longed for suffering, longed for my blood to be drained – drop by drop in these sufferings. But they just laughed at me and finally came to regard me as a saintly fool. They made excuses for me, saying that they had received only what they had been asking for, and that all they had now could not have been otherwise. At last they declared that I was becoming a danger to them, and that they would lock me up in the madhouse if I did not keep quiet. At this, sorrow gripped my heart so fiercely that I could not breathe, I felt that I was dying, and then . . . that was when I woke up.

It was already day, or rather day had not yet dawned but it was after five. I awoke in my armchair; my candle had burnt out, the captain's room was locked in sleep, and a silence unusual for our house reigned about me. I instantly leapt to my feet in amazement: nothing even remotely like this had ever happened to me before, not in any of the trifling details that did not really matter such as falling asleep in my chair, for instance. And suddenly, as I stood there recovering my senses, I saw my revolver lying all ready and loaded before me. With a quick thrust I pushed it away. No, give me life now, life! I raised my arms and invoked the eternal Truth, or rather wept, for all my being was roused to exultation, immeasurable exultation. Yes, I wanted to live and spread the word. My resolution to preach came on the instant, to preach now and for ever, of course. I shall preach, I must preach – what? Truth. For I have seen it, seen it with my own eyes, seen it in all its glory.

And so I have been spreading the word ever since. What is more, the ones who laugh at me are dearer to me now than all the others. Why it is so I do not know nor can explain, but let it be so. They say that I am floundering already, that is, if I am floundering so badly now how do I expect to go on? It's perfectly true, I am floundering and it may become even worse as I go on. There is no doubt that I will indeed flounder and lose my way more than once before I learn how best to preach, that is with what words and by what deeds, for it is a very difficult mission. It's all as clear as day to me even now, you know; but, listen, who of us does not flounder? And yet everyone is going towards the same thing, at least all strive for the same thing, all – from the wise man to the meanest wretch – only all follow different paths. It's an old truth, but here's something new: I cannot flounder too badly, you know. Because I have seen the Truth, I have seen it and I know that people can be beautiful and happy without losing their ability to dwell on this earth. I cannot and will not believe that evil is man's natural state. And yet it's just this conviction of mine that makes them all laugh at me. How could I help believing it, though: I have seen the Truth, it was not a figment of my imagination or my mind, I have seen it, seen it, and its *living image* has taken hold of my soul for ever. I have seen it in such consummate wholeness that I refuse to believe that it cannot live among men. And so, how could I lose my way? I shall stray once or twice of course, I shall perhaps even use the words of others sometimes, but not for long: the living image of what I have seen will remain with me always, it will always correct me and put me straight. I am full of vigour and strength. I shall go and preach, be it for a thousand years. Do you know, I first wanted to conceal the fact that I had corrupted them all, but that would have been a mistake – a mistake already, you see. Truth whispered in my ear that I was *lying*, Truth saved me and showed me the way. But I do not know how to build a paradise on earth, for I do not know how to put it in words. I lost the words on awakening. At least all the most important words, the most essential. Never mind; I shall go on my way and preach tirelessly, because I have seen it with my own eyes, even though I cannot describe what I have seen. That is something the mockers fail to understand. They say: 'It was just a dream, ravings and hallucinations.' Oh dear! Is that clever? And they are so proud of themselves, too. A dream, they say. But what is a dream? Isn't our life a dream? I shall go further: let it never, never come true, let paradise never be (after all, I do realise that!) I shall anyway go and spread the word. And yet it could be done so simply: in a single day, *in a single hour* everything would be settled! One should love others as one loves oneself, that is the main thing, that is all, nothing else, absolutely nothing else is needed, and then one would instantly know how to go about it. It's nothing but an old truth, repeated and read billions of times, and yet it has not taken root. 'Consciousness of life is superior to life, knowledge of the laws of happiness is superior to happiness' – this is what we must fight against. And I shall. If only everyone wanted it, it could be all done at once.

As for that little girl, I have found her . . . And I shall go on! Yes, I shall go on!

– *Anna Karenina* as a Fact of
Special Importance –

(July and August 1877)

A nd so, at that very time – one evening last
spring, that is – I happened to meet one of my
favourite writers on the street. We meet rarely, once
every few months, and somehow always by chance on
the street. He is one of the most prominent among
those five or six writers who are usually called the
'Pleiade,' for some reason. The critics, at least, have
followed the readers and have set them apart and
placed them above all the other writers; this has been
the case for some time now – still the same group of
five, and the Pleiade's membership does not increase.
I enjoy meeting this dear novelist of whom I am so
fond; I enjoy showing him, among other things, that I
think he is quite wrong in saying that he has become
old-fashioned and will write nothing more. I always
bring away some subtle and perceptive insight from
our brief conversations. We had much to talk about
this time, for the war had already begun. But he at
once began speaking directly about *Anna Karenina*. I
had also just finished reading part seven, with which
the novel had concluded in *The Russian Messenger*.
My interlocutor does not look like a man of strong

enthusiasms. On this occasion, however, I was struck by the firmness and passionate insistence of his views on *Anna Karenina*.

'It's something unprecedented, a first. Are there any of our writers who could rival it? Could anyone imagine anything like it in Europe? Is there any work in all their literatures over the past years, and even much earlier, that could stand next to it?'

What struck me most in this verdict, which I myself shared completely, was that the mention of Europe was so relevant to those very questions and problems that were arising of their own accord in the minds of so many. The book at once took on, in my eyes, the dimensions of a fact that could give Europe an answer on our behalf, that long-sought-after fact we could show to Europe. Of course, people will howl and scoff that this is only a work of literature, some sort of novel, and that it's absurd to exaggerate this way and go off to Europe carrying only a novel. I know that people will howl and scoff, but don't worry: I'm not exaggerating and am looking at the matter soberly: I know very well that this is still only a novel and that it's but a tiny drop of what we need; but the main thing for me here is that this drop already exists, it is given, it really and truly does exist; and so, if we already have it, if the Russian genius could give birth to this *fact*, then it is not doomed to impotence and can create; it can provide something *of its own*, it can begin *its own* word and finish uttering it when the times and seasons come to pass. And besides, this is much more than a mere drop. Oh, I'm not exaggerating here either: I know very well that you won't find, either in any individual member of this Pleiade or in the whole Pleiade together, anything that can be called, strictly speaking, a creative force of true genius. In our entire literature there have been but three unquestioned geniuses who had an unquestionably 'new word' to utter, and these three were Lomonosov, Pushkin, and, in part, Gogol. This whole Pleiade (including the author of *Anna Karenina*) emerged directly from Pushkin, one of the greatest of Russians who, however, is still far from being interpreted and understood properly. There are two principal ideas in Pushkin, and they both contain a model of the whole of Russia's future mission and goal, and therefore of our whole future destiny. The first is Russia's *universality*, her capacity to respond, and the genuine, unquestioned, profound kinship of her genius with the geniuses of all ages and all peoples of the world. Pushkin does not merely call our attention to this idea or convey it in the form of a doctrine or theory or as a cherished hope or prophecy; he carries it out *in practice*, embodies it, and proves it forever in his brilliant creations. He is a man of the ancient world; he is also a German and an Englishman, deeply aware of his own animating spirit and the anguish of his aspirations ('A Feast in Time of Plague'); he is a poet of the East. To all these peoples he stated and proclaimed that the Russian genius knew them, has understood them, has

111

touched them like a brother, that it can fully *reincarnate* itself in them, that to the Russian spirit alone is given universality and the future mission to comprehend and to unify all the diverse nationalities and to eliminate all their contradictions. Pushkin's other idea was his turning to the People and investing his hopes in their strength alone, his pledge that in the People and in the People alone will we fully discover our whole Russian genius and our consciousness of its mission. And here, too, Pushkin did not merely point out a fact but was also the first to realise the fact in practice. It was only with him that we began our real, conscious turn to the People, something that had been inconceivable before him ever since Peter's reforms. The whole Pleiade of today have worked only along his lines; after Pushkin no one has said anything *new*. All their sources were in him, and he pointed them out. And besides, the Pleiade has elaborated only the tiniest part of what he pointed out. What they have done, however, has been done with such largess of talent, with such depth and distinction, that Pushkin would naturally have acknowledged them.

The idea behind *Anna Karenina*, of course, is nothing new or unheard of in Russia. Instead of this novel we could, of course, show Europe the source – Pushkin himself, that is – as the strongest, most vivid, and most incontestable proof of the independence of the Russian genius and its rights to a great, worldwide, pan-human and all-unifying significance in the future.

(Alas, no matter how we tried to show them that, Europe will not read our writers for a long time yet; and if Europe does begin to read them, the Europeans will not be able to understand and appreciate them for a long time. Indeed, they are utterly unable to appreciate our writers, not because of insufficient capacity, but because for them we are an entirely different world, just as if we had come down from the moon, so that it is difficult for them even to admit the fact that we exist. All this I know, and I speak of 'showing Europe' only in the sense of our own conviction of our right to independence vis-à-vis Europe.) Nevertheless, *Anna Karenina* is perfection as a work of art that appeared at just the right moment and as a work to which nothing in the European literatures of this era can compare; and, in the second place, the novel's idea also contains something of ours, something truly *our own*, namely that very thing which constitutes our distinctness from the European world, the thing which constitutes our 'new word,' or at least its beginnings – just the kind of word one cannot hear in Europe, yet one that Europe still so badly needs, despite all her pride.

I cannot embark upon literary criticism here and will say only a few things. *Anna Karenina* expresses a view of human guilt and transgression. People are shown living under abnormal conditions. Evil existed before they did. Caught up in a whirl of falsities, people transgress and are doomed to destruction. As you can see, it is one of the oldest and most popular of

European themes. But how is such a problem solved in Europe? Generally in Europe there are two ways of solving it. Solution number one: the law has been given, recorded, formulated, and put together through the course of millennia. Good and evil have been defined and weighed, their extent and degree have been determined historically by humanity's wise men, by unceasing work on the human soul, and by working out, in a very scientific manner, the extent of the forces that unite people in a society. One is commanded to follow this elaborated code of laws blindly. He who does not follow it, he who transgresses, pays with his freedom, his property, or his life; he pays literally and cruelly. 'I know,' says their civilisation, 'that this is blind and cruel and impossible, since we are not able to work out the ultimate formula for humanity while we are still at the midpoint of its journey; but since we have no other solution, it follows that we must hold to that which is written, and hold to it literally and cruelly. Without it, things would be even worse. At the same time, despite all the abnormality and absurdity of the structure we call our great European civilisation, let the forces of the human spirit remain healthy and intact; let society not be shaken in its faith that it is moving toward perfection; let no one dare think that the idea of the beautiful and sublime has been obscured, that the concepts of good and evil are being distorted and twisted, that convention is constantly taking the place of the healthy norm, that simplicity and naturalness are perishing as they are crushed by a constant accumulation of lies!'

The second solution is the reverse: 'Since society is arranged in an abnormal manner, one cannot demand that human entities be responsible for the consequences of their actions. Therefore, the criminal is not responsible, and crime at present does not exist. In order to put an end to crime and human guilt we must put an end to the abnormality of society and its structure. Since curing the ills in the existing order of things is a long and hopeless process, and the medicines needed have not even been found, it follows that the whole society must be destroyed and the old order swept away with a broom, as it were. Then we can begin it all anew, on different principles as yet unknown but which, nevertheless, can be no worse than those of the present order; on the contrary, they offer many chances of success. Our main hope is in science.' And so this is the second solution: they wait for the future ant heap and in the meantime will wet the earth with blood. The world of western Europe offers no other solutions for guilt and human transgression.

The Russian author's view of guilt and transgression recognises that no ant heap, no triumph of the 'fourth estate,' no abolition of poverty, no organisation of labor will save humanity from abnormality and, consequently, from guilt and transgression. This is expressed in a monumental psychological elaboration of the human soul, with awesome depth and force and with a realism of artistic portrayal unprecedented among us. It is clear and intelligible to the point of obviousness that evil lies deeper in human beings than our socialist-physicians suppose; that no social structure will eliminate evil; that the human soul will remain as it always has been; that abnormality and sin arise from that soul itself; and, finally, that the laws of the human soul are still so little known, so obscure to science, so undefined, and so mysterious, that there are not and cannot be either physicians or *final* judges; but there is He who says: 'Vengeance is mine, I will repay.' He alone knows *all* the mystery of this world and the final destiny of man. Humans themselves still cannot venture to decide anything with pride in infallibility; the times and the seasons for that have not yet arrived. The human judge himself ought to know that he is not the final judge; that he himself is a sinner; that the measure and the scales in his hands will be an absurdity *if* he, holding that measure and scales, does not himself submit to the law of the yet unsolved mystery and turn to the only solution – to Mercy and Love. And so that man might not perish in despair and ignorance of his path and destiny, of his conviction of evil's mysterious and fateful inevitability, he has been shown a way out. This the poet has brilliantly shown in a masterful scene in the novel's penultimate part, in the scene of the heroine's mortal illness, when the transgressors and enemies are suddenly transformed into higher beings, into brothers who have forgiven one another everything, into beings who, through mutual forgiveness, have cast off lies, guilt, and crime and thereby at once have absolved themselves with full awareness of their right to absolution. But later, at the end of the novel, we have a gloomy and terrible picture of the full degeneration of a human spirit; this we follow step by step through the depiction of that compelling state in which evil, having taken possession of a human being, trammels his every movement and paralyses every effort toward resistance, every thought, every wish to struggle with the darkness that falls upon the soul; deliberately, eagerly, with a passion for vengeance, the soul accepts the darkness instead of the light. In this picture there is such a profound lesson for the human judge, for the one who holds the measure and the scales, that he will naturally exclaim in fear and perplexity, 'No, vengeance is not always mine, and it is not always for me to repay.' And the human judge will not cruelly charge the grievously fallen criminal with having scorned the light of the age-old solution and with having *deliberately* rejected it. He will not, at least, cling to the letter of the law . . .

If we have literary works of such power of thought and execution, then why can we not *eventually* have *our own* science as well, and our own economic and social solutions? Why does Europe refuse us our independence, *our own* word? These are questions that cannot help but be asked. It would be absurd to suppose that nature has endowed us only with literary talents. All the other things are a matter of history, circumstances, and the conditions of the time. Our own homegrown Europeans, at least, ought to be thinking this way while they await the judgment of the European Europeans . . .

– A Lie Is Saved by a Lie –
(September 1877)

O nce upon a time Don Quixote – that very well-
known knight of the doleful countenance, the
noblest of all the knights the world has ever seen, the
simplest in soul and one of the greatest in heart – while
wandering with his faithful attendant, Sancho, in
search of adventure, was suddenly struck by a puzzle
that gave him cause to think for a long while. The fact
is that often the knights of old, beginning with Amadis
da Gaula, whose stories have come down to us in the
absolutely truthful books known as the romances of
chivalry (for acquisition of which Don Quixote did not
regret selling several of the best acres of his little estate) – often these knights, during their glorious pere-
grinations that were so beneficial to the whole world,
would suddenly and unexpectedly encounter entire
armies of even a hundred thousand warriors sent forth
against them by some evil power, by evil sorcerers who
envied them and prevented them in all sorts of ways
from achieving their great goal and being united at last
with their fair ladies. It usually happened that when a
knight encountered such a monstrous and evil army he
would draw his sword, invoke the name of his fair lady
for spiritual succour, and then hack his way into the

very midst of his enemies, whom he would annihilate to the last man. This would seem to be quite a simple matter, but Don Quixote suddenly fell to thinking, and on this problem: he suddenly found it impossible to believe that a single knight, no matter how strong he might be and no matter if he were to go on wielding his armipotent sword for a whole day without getting tired, could at once lay low a hundred thousand enemies, and this in only one battle. Killing each man would still take some time; killing a hundred thousand men would take a great deal of time; and no matter how he wielded his sword, a single person could not do this at once, in a few hours or so. And yet these trustworthy books told of such deeds being done in just a single battle. How could it happen?

'I have solved this puzzle, Sancho, my friend,' Don Quixote said at last. 'Inasmuch as all these giants, all these wicked sorcerers, were the evil spirit, their armies likewise possessed the same magical and evil nature. I presume that these armies were composed of men quite unlike you and me, for instance. These men were no more than an illusion, the product of magic, and in all probability their bodies were unlike our own but were more akin to those of slugs, worms, and spiders, for example. And thus in his powerful hand the knight's steadfast and sharp sword would, when it fell upon these bodies, pass through them in an instant, almost without resistance, as if through air. And if that is so, then truly with a single blow he could cut through three or four bodies, and even through ten if they were standing close together. Hence one can understand that the thing would be greatly expedited and a knight really could annihilate whole armies of such evil blackamoors and other monsters . . .'

Here the great poet and seer of the human heart perceived one of the most profound and most mysterious aspects of the human spirit. Oh, this is a great book, not the sort that are written now; only one such book is sent to humanity in several hundred years. And such perceptions of the profoundest aspects of human nature you will find on every page of this book. Take only the fact that this Sancho, the personification of common sense, prudence, cunning, the golden mean, has chanced to become a friend and traveling companion to the maddest person on earth – he precisely, and no other! He deceives him the whole time, he cheats him like a child, and yet he has complete faith in his great intellect, is enchanted to the point of tenderness by the greatness of his heart, believes completely in all the preposterous dreams of the great knight, and the whole time he never once doubts that the Don will at last conquer the island for him! What a fine thing it would be if our young people were to become thoroughly steeped in these great works of world literature. I don't know what is now being taught in courses of literature, but a knowledge of this most splendid and sad of all books created by human genius would certainly elevate the soul of a young person with a great idea, give rise to profound questions in his heart, and work toward diverting his mind from worship of the eternal and foolish idol of mediocrity, self-satisfied conceit, and cheap prudence. Man will not forget to take this *saddest* of all books with him to God's last judgment. He will point to the most profound and fateful mystery of humans and humankind that the book conveys. He will point to the fact that humanity's most sublime beauty, its most sublime purity, chastity, forthrightness, gentleness, courage, and, finally, its most sublime intellect – all these often (alas, all too often) come to naught, pass without benefit to humanity, and even become an object of humanity's derision simply because all these most noble and precious gifts with which a person is often endowed lack but the very last gift – that of *genius* to put all this power to work and to direct it along a path of action that is truthful, not fantastic and insane, so as to work for the benefit of humanity! But genius, alas, is given out to the tribes and the peoples in such small quantities and so rarely that the spectacle of the malicious irony of fate that so often dooms the efforts of some of the noblest of people and the most ardent friends of humanity to scorn and laughter and to the casting of stones solely because these people, at the fateful moment, were unable to discern the true sense of things and so discover their *new word* – this spectacle of the needless ruination of such great and noble forces actually may reduce a friend of humanity to despair, evoke not laughter but bitter tears and sour his heart, hitherto pure and believing, with doubt . . .

However, I wanted only to point out this most interesting feature which, along with hundreds of other such profound perceptions, Cervantes revealed in the human heart. The most preposterous of people, with a crackpot belief in the most preposterous fantasy anyone can conceive, suddenly falls into doubt and perplexity that almost shake his entire faith. What's curious is the thing that was able to shake it: not the absurdity of the crackpot notion itself, not the absurdity of wandering knights who exist for the benefit of humanity, not the absurdity of those magical wonders told of in those 'absolutely truthful books' – no, on the contrary, it was something external and secondary, an altogether particular thing. The preposterous man suddenly *began yearning for realism*! It wasn't the appearance of sorcerers' armies that bothered him: oh, that's beyond any doubt; and how else could these great and splendid knights display all their valour if they were not visited by all these trials, if there were no envious giants and wicked sorcerers? The ideal of the wandering knight is so great, so beautiful and useful, and had so captivated the heart of the noble Don Quixote that it became utterly impossible for him to renounce his faith in it; that would have been the equivalent of betraying his ideal, his duty, his love for Dulcinea and for humanity. (When he did renounce his ideal, when he was cured of his madness and grew *wiser*, after returning from his second campaign in which he was defeated by the wise and commonsensical barber Carrasco, the skeptic and debunker, he promptly passed away, quietly, with a sad smile, consoling the weeping Sancho, loving the whole world with the mighty force of love contained in his sacred heart, and yet realizing that there was nothing more for him to do in this world.) No, it was not that; what troubled him was merely the very real, mathematical consideration that no matter how the knight might wield his sword and no matter how strong he might be, he still could not overcome an army of a hundred thousand in the course of a few hours, or even in a day, having killed all of them to the last man. And yet such things were written in these trustworthy books. Therefore, they must have lied. And if there is one lie, then it is all a lie. How, then, can *truth* be saved? And so, to save the truth he invents another fantasy; but this one is twice, thrice as fantastic as the first one, cruder and more absurd; he invents hundreds of thousands of imaginary men having the bodies of slugs, which the knight's keen blade can pass through ten times more easily and quickly than it can an ordinary human body. And thus realism is satisfied, truth is saved, and it's possible to believe in the first and most important dream with no more doubts – and all this, again, is solely thanks to the second, even more absurd fantasy, invented only to salvage the *realism* of the first one.

Ask yourselves: hasn't the same thing happened to you, perhaps, a hundred times in the course of your life? Say you've come to cherish a certain dream, an idea, a theory, a conviction, or some external fact that struck you, or, at last, a woman who has enchanted you. You rush off in pursuit of the object of your love with all the intensity your soul can muster. It's true that no matter how blinded you may be, no matter how well your heart bribes you, still, if in the object of your love there is a lie, a *delusion*, something that you yourself have exaggerated and distorted because of your passion and your initial rush of feeling – solely so that you can make it your idol and bow down to it – then, of course, you're aware of it in the depths of your being; doubt weighs upon your mind and teases it, ranges through your soul and prevents you from living peaceably with your beloved dream. Now, don't you remember, won't you admit even to yourself what it was that suddenly set your mind at rest? Didn't you invent a new dream, a new lie, even a terribly crude one, perhaps, but one that you were quick to embrace lovingly only because it resolved your initial doubt?

– Pushkin (A Sketch) –
(August 1880)

*Excerpt from a speech delivered on June 8, 1880 at a Meeting
of the Society of Lovers of Russian Literature*

. . . Everywhere in Pushkin we perceive a faith in the
Russian character, a faith in its spiritual power; and if
there is faith, then there must be hope as well, a great
hope for the Russian: 'With hopes for glory and for
good, / I look ahead and have no fear,' said the poet
himself when speaking of another subject; but these
words of his can be applied directly to the whole of his
creative activity drawn from his nation. And never has
any Russian writer, before him or since, been so akin
in spirit to his People as was Pushkin. Oh, we have
many experts on the People among our writers, ones
who write with such talent, so aptly and so lovingly
about the People; and yet if one compares them with
Pushkin, they are, truly (with perhaps two exceptions
from his latest followers), merely 'gentlemen' who
write about the People. The most talented of these,
even these two exceptions I just mentioned, will now
and then suddenly show a haughty attitude, something
from another world and another way of life, something
that shows a wish to raise the People to their own level
and make them happy by doing so. In Pushkin there

is precisely something that truly makes him akin to the People, something that reaches almost the level of simple-hearted tenderness. Take his 'Tale of the Bear' and the peasant who killed his 'lady bear,' or recall the verses 'Brother Ivan, when you and I start drinking,' and you will see what I mean.

Our great poet left all these treasures of art and artistic vision as signposts for the artists who came after him and for those who would toil in the same fields as he. One can positively state that had Pushkin not existed neither would the talented people who came after him. At least they, despite their great gifts, would not have made their presence felt with such power and clarity of expression as they did later, in our time. But the point is not merely in poetry and not merely in creative work: had Pushkin not existed, it might well be that our faith in our Russian individuality, our now conscious hope in the strength of our People, and with it our faith in our future independent mission in the family of European peoples would not have been formulated with such unshakeable force (this did happen later, but was by no means universal and was felt by merely a few). This feat of Pushkin's becomes particularly evident if one studies what I call the third period of his creative work.

Once more, I repeat: these periods do not have such firm boundaries. Some of the works of even this third period could have appeared at the very beginning of our poet's career, because Pushkin was always a complete, integrated organism, so to say, an organism bearing all its beginnings within itself and not acquiring them from without. The outside world only aroused in him those things already stored in the depths of his soul. But this organism did develop, and the particular nature of each of the periods of this development actually can be shown and the gradual progression from one period to the next indicated. Thus, to the third period belongs the series of works in which universal ideas shine forth most brightly, which reflect the poetic images of other nations and which incarnate their genius. Some of these works appeared only posthumously. And in this period of his career our poet stands forth as an almost miraculous and unprecedented phenomenon, never before seen anywhere else. In fact, the European literatures had creative geniuses of immense magnitude – the Shakespeares, Cervanteses, and Schillers. But show me even one of these great geniuses who possessed the capacity to respond to the whole world that our Pushkin had. And it is this capacity, the principal capacity of our nationality, that he shares with our People; and it is this, above all, that makes him a national poet. The very greatest of these European poets could never exemplify as intensely as Pushkin the genius of another people – even a people that might be near at hand – the spirit of that people, all the hidden depths of that spirit and all its longing to fulfill its destiny. On the contrary, when the European poets dealt with other nationalities they most often instilled in them their own nationality and interpreted them from their own national standpoint. Even Shakespeare's Italians, for instance, are almost to a man the same as Englishmen. Pushkin alone, of all the poets of the world, possesses the quality of embodying himself fully within another nationality. Take his 'Scenes from Faust,' his 'Covetous Knight,' his ballad 'Once There Lived a Poor Knight.' Read 'Don Juan' once more, and were it not for Pushkin's name on it you would never guess that it had not been written by a Spaniard. What profound, fantastic images there are in the poem 'A Feast in Time of Plague!' But in these fantastic images you hear the genius of England; this marvellous song sung by the poem's hero about the plague, this song of Mary with the verses, 'Once the noisy school rang out, / With the voices of our children,' these English songs, this longing of the British genius, this lament, this agonizing presentiment of the future. Just recall the strange verses: 'Once, wandering 'midst a valley wild . . .'

This is almost a literal reworking of the first three pages of a strange, mystical book written in prose by one ancient English religious sectarian – but is it merely a reworking? In the melancholy and rapturous music of these verses one senses the very soul of northern Protestantism, of an English heresiarch whose mysticism knows no bounds, with his dull, gloomy, and compelling strivings and with all the unchecked force of mystical visions. Reading these strange verses, you seem to sense the spirit of the age of the Reformation; you begin to understand this militant fire of incipient Protestantism; you begin to understand, finally, the history itself, and understand it not only rationally but as though you had been there yourself, had passed through the armed camp of sectarians, sung hymns with them, wept with them in their mystical ecstasies, and shared their beliefs. Incidentally, right next to this religious mysticism we find other religious stanzas from the Koran, or 'Imitations of the Koran': do we not find a real Moslem here? Is this not the very spirit of the Koran and its sword, the simple-hearted majesty of the faith and its awesome, bloody power? And here, too, we find the ancient world – 'The Egyptian Nights'; here we see these earthly gods, who have been enthroned as divinities over their people, who despise the very spirit of their people and its aspirations, who no longer believe in it, who have become solitary gods in truth and who have gone mad in their isolation, who in their anguish and weariness while waiting to die seek diversion in outrageous brutalities, in insect-like voluptuousness, the voluptuousness of a female spider devouring her mate. No, I will say positively that there has not been a poet so able to respond to the whole world as Pushkin; and the point is not only in this ability to respond but in its astounding depth and in his ability to infuse his spirit into the spirit of other nations, something that was almost complete and so was marvellous as well, because nowhere in any other poet anywhere in the world has such a phenomenon been repeated. This we find only in Pushkin, and in this sense, I repeat, he is unprecedented and, in my view, prophetic, for . . . for it was just here that his national Russian strength was most fully expressed, that the national spirit of his poetry was expressed, the national spirit as it will develop in the future, the national spirit of our future, already concealed within our present and expressed prophetically. For what is the strength of the spirit of Russianness if not its ultimate aspirations toward universality and the universal brotherhood of peoples? Having become completely a national poet, Pushkin at once, as soon as he came in contact with the force of the People, at once senses the great future mission of this force. Here he is a visionary; here he is a prophet.

In fact, what did Peter's reform mean for us, not only in terms of the future but even in terms of what has already happened and already is evident to all? What was the significance of this reform for us? It meant not only our adopting European clothing, customs, inventions, and European science. Let us try to understand what happened and look into it more closely. Indeed, it is quite possible that Peter first began to carry out his reform in just this sense, that is to say, in an immediately utilitarian sense; but subsequently, in his further development of his idea, Peter undoubtedly followed a certain secret instinct that led him to work toward future goals that certainly were im-

mensely broader than mere immediate utilitarianism.
The Russian People as well accepted the reforms in
just the same spirit – not merely one of utilitarianism
but having certainly sensed almost at once some further and incomparably more elevated goal than immediate utilitarianism; I must repeat, of course, that they
sensed that goal unconsciously, yet also directly and as
something absolutely vital. It was then that we at once
began to strive toward a truly vital reunification, toward the universal brotherhood of peoples! It was not
with hostility (as should have been the case, it would
seem) but with friendship and complete love that we
accepted the genius of other nations into our soul, all
of them together, making no discriminations by race,
knowing instinctively almost from our very first step
where the distinctions lay, knowing how to eliminate
contradictions, to excuse and reconcile differences;
and in so doing we revealed the quality that had only
just been made manifest – our readiness and our in-
clination for the general reunification of all people of
all the tribes of the great Aryan race. Indeed, the mission of the Russian is unquestionably pan-European
and universal. To become a real Russian, to become
completely Russian, perhaps, means just (in the final
analysis – please bear that in mind) to become a brother to all people, a *panhuman*, if you like. Oh, all our
Slavophilism and Westernising is no more than one
great misunderstanding between us, although it was
historically necessary. To a real Russian, Europe and

the lot of all the great Aryan tribe are just as dear as is Russia herself, as is the lot of our own native land, because our lot is universality, achieved not through the sword but through the strength of brotherhood and our brotherly aspirations toward the unity of people. If you care to look closely into our history after the Petrine reforms, you will already find traces and indications of this idea – this vision of mine, if you wish to call it that – in the way we dealt with the peoples of Europe, even in our official policy. For what was Russia doing in her policy over these whole two centuries if not serving Europe, far more, perhaps, than she was serving herself? I do not think that this happened merely through the ineptness of our politicians. Oh, the nations of Europe simply do not know how dear they are to us! And subsequently, I am certain, we (I mean not we, of course, but Russian people to come) will realize to the very last man that to become a genuine Russian will mean specifically: to strive to bring an ultimate reconciliation to Europe's contradictions, to indicate that the solution to Europe's anguish is to be found in the panhuman and all-unifying Russian soul, to enfold all our brethren within it with brotherly love, and at last, perhaps, to utter the ultimate word of great, general harmony, ultimate brotherly accord of all tribes through the law of Christ's Gospel!

I know, I know full well that my words may seem ecstatic, exaggerated, and fantastic. So be it: but I do not regret having said them. This had to be said, and particularly now, at the moment of our celebration, at the moment we pay honour to our great genius who embodied this very idea in his artistic power. And, indeed, this idea has been expressed more than once; I have said nothing new. What is most important is that all this might seem conceited: 'Is it for us,' some may say, 'for our impoverished, crude land to have such a destiny? Can it be we who are ordained to utter a new word to humanity?' But, after all, am I speaking about economic prominence, about the glory of the sword or science? I am speaking merely of the brotherhood of people and of the fact that, perhaps, the Russian heart is most plainly destined, among all the peoples, for universally human and brotherly unity; I see traces of this in our history, in our gifted people, in the artistic genius of Pushkin. Our land may be impoverished, but this impoverished land 'Christ Himself, in slavish garb, traversed and gave His blessing.' Why can we not accommodate His ultimate word? Was He not born in a manger Himself? I repeat: at the very least we can now point to Pushkin and to the universality and panhumanness of his genius. He could accommodate the geniuses of other nations within his soul as if they were his own. In art, in his artistic work, at least, he showed beyond dispute this universal striving of the Russian spirit, and that in itself reveals something important. If my idea is a fantasy, then in Pushkin, at least, there is something on which this fantasy can be founded. Had he lived longer, perhaps, he would have shown us immortal and grand images of the Russian soul that could have been understood by our European brethren and might have attracted them to us much more and much more closely than now; he might have managed to explain to them the whole truth of our aspirations, and they would have understood us more clearly than they do now; they would have begun to divine our purpose; they would have ceased to regard us as mistrustfully and haughtily as they do now. Had Pushkin lived longer, perhaps there would be fewer misunderstandings and disputes among us than we see now. But God did not will it so. Pushkin died in the full flower of his creative development, and unquestionably he took some great secret with him to his grave. And so now we must puzzle out this secret without him.

FURTHER READING

Bird, Robert, *Fyodor Dostoevsky* (Critical Lives), Reaktion (2012)

Catteau, J. *Dostoyevsky and the Process of Literary Creation*, tr. A. Littlewood, Cambridge University Press (1989)

Frank, Joseph, *Dostoevsky: The Seeds of Revolt, 1821–1849*, Princeton University Press (1976)

— *Dostoevsky: The Years of Ordeal, 1850–1859* (1983)

— *Dostoevsky: The Stir of Liberation, 1860–1865* (1986)

— *Dostoevsky: The Miraculous Years, 1865–1871* (1995)

— *Dostoevsky: The Mantle of the Prophet, 1871–1881* (2002)

— *Dostoevsky: A Writer in His Time* (2012)

Gibson, A. Boyce, *The Religion of Dostoevsky*, SCM Press (1973)

Hudspith, Sarah, *Dostoevsky and the Idea of Russianness*, Routledge Curzon (2004)

Ivanits, Linda, *Dostoevsky and the Russian People*, Cambridge University Press (2008)

Jackson, Robert Louis, *The Art of Dostoevsky: Deliriums and Nocturnes*, Princeton University Press (1981)

Kjetsaa, Geir, *Fyodor Dostoyevsky, A Writer's Life*, tr. Siri Hustvedt and David McDuff, Viking (1987)

Lantz, Kenneth, *The Dostoevsky Encyclopedia*, Greenwood Press (2004)

Leatherbarrow, W. J., ed., *The Cambridge Companion to Dostoevsky*, Cambridge University Press (2002)

Martinsen, Deborah A., ed., *Literary Journals in Imperial Russia*, Cambridge University Press (1997)

Martinsen, Deborah A., and Olga Maiorova, eds.,
Dostoevsky in Context, Cambridge University Press (2015)

Miller, Robin Feuer, *Dostoevsky's Unfinished Journey*, Yale
University Press (2007)

Morson, Gary Saul, *The Boundaries of Genre: Dostoevsky's
'Diary of a Writer' and the Traditions of Literary Utopia*,
University of Texas Press (1981)

— 'Introductory Study: Dostoevsky's Great Experiment',
in *Fyodor Dostoevsky, A Writer's Diary*, 2 vols, tr. and
annotated by Kenneth Lantz, Northwestern University
Press (1993–4)

Paperno, Irina, *Suicide as a Cultural Institution in
Dostoevsky's Russia*, Cornell University Press (1997)

Scanlan, James P., *Dostoevsky the Thinker*, Cornell
University Press (2002)

Vassena, Raffaella, *Reawakening Russian Identity:
Dostoevsky's 'Diary of a Writer' and its Impact on Russian
Society*, Peter Lang (2007)

Volgin, Igor, 'Poverkh bar'erov. Zagadka *Dnevnika pisatelya*'
[Over The Barriers. The Mystery of *A Writer's Diary*],
introduction to Dostoevskii, F. M., *Dnevnik pisatelya*,
2 vols ['first complete scholarly edition, published to
commemorate the 190th anniversary of Dostoevsky's
birth'], commentary (vol. 1) by V. Rak, A. Arkhipova, G.
Galagan, E. Kiiko, V. Tunimanov, (vol. 2) by A. Batyuto,
A. Berezkin, V. Vetlovskaya, E. Kiiko, G. Stepanova, V.
Tunimanov, Knizhnyi Klub (2011)

Other titles from Notting Hill Editions*

A Short History of Power
by Simon Heffer

Taking a panoramic view from the days of Thucydides to the present, Heffer analyses the motive forces behind the pursuit of power, and explains in a beautiful argument why history is destined to repeat itself.

'Heffer's admirably steely tract combines a well-informed history intelligence with a subtle account of 2,500 years of Western history.' – *Times Literary Supplement*

The Mystery of Being Human: God, Freedom and the NHS
by Raymond Tallis

In his latest collection of essays, author, physician and humanist philosopher Raymond Tallis meditates on the complexity of human consciousness, free will, mathematics, God and eternity. The philosophical reflections are interrupted by a fierce polemic 'Lord Howe's Wicked Dream', in which Tallis exposes the 'institutionally corrupt' deception intended to destroy the NHS.

Pilgrims of the Air: The Passing of the Passenger Pigeons
by John Wilson Foster

This is the story of the rapid and brutal extinction of the Passenger Pigeon, once so abundant that they 'blotted out the sky', until the last bird died on 1st September, 1914. It is also an evocative story of wild America – the astonishment that accompanied its discovery, the allure of its natural 'productions', its ruthless exploitation, and a morality tale for our times.

CLASSIC COLLECTION

The Classic Collection brings together the finest essayists of the past, introduced by contemporary writers.

*All NHE titles are available in the UK, and some titles are available in the rest of the world. For more information, please visit www.nottinghilleditions.com.

A selection of our titles is distributed in the US and Canada by New York Review Books. For more information on available titles, please visit www.nyrb.com.